IMPAWSIBLE MISCHIEF

THE SPELLWOOD WITCHES, BOOK 4

MELANIE SNOW

Spirit Paw Press, LLC

CONTENTS

Also by Melanie Snow   v
Thank You   vii

Chapter 1   1
Chapter 2   18
Chapter 3   34
Chapter 4   49
Chapter 5   66
Chapter 6   80
Chapter 7   92
Chapter 8   103
Chapter 9   126
Chapter 10   137
Chapter 11   144
Chapter 12   153
Chapter 13   173
Chapter 14   193
Chapter 15   209
Chapter 16   214
Chapter 17   218

A Note from Melanie   225
Pawtrayal, Book 5   227
Enjoy an Excerpt from Pawtrayal   229
Pawtrayal   231
Discover The Spellwood Witches   237
Don't Miss Your Free Gift!   241
About Melanie Snow   243
How to Find Melanie Snow   245
Acknowledgements   247

The Spellwood Witches Series

Witch's Tail
Howl Play
Tail of a Feather
Impawsible Mischief
Pawtrayal

Impawsible Mischief

The Spellwood Witches, Book 4

This is a work of fiction. Names, characters, places, and incidents are a product of the author's imagination. Locales and public names are sometimes used for atmospheric purposes. Any resemblance to actual people, living or dead, or to businesses, companies, events, institutions, or locales is completely coincidental.

ASIN: B08PC8GCVQ

ISBN: 978-1-7324375-9-3

(Spirit Paw Press, LLC, Concord, NH 03303)

www.wendyvandepoll.com/melanie-snow

Thank You

Download Your Free Gift

A Welcome to Witchland Map

Thank you for purchasing *Impawsible Mischief, The Spellwood Witches, Book 4*. To show my appreciation and because of a popular request from my readers I am offering a:

Welcome to Witchland Map

https://wendyvandepoll.com/melaniesnowgift

"It's such a nice day," Sarah Spellwood said, happily breathing in the rich fragrance of flowers that had permeated Witchland's atmosphere.

The first green shoots had started to break through the ground and dust the trees, and now Hua's gardens and the town's gardens were erupting in full bloom. Witchland always blossomed earlier than anywhere else in New Hampshire, Hua had explained to her, largely thanks to the Leekins, the small faeries populating the woods and spreading their plant magic to keep the area verdant. Their spells caused the crocuses to spring up through the snow in startling shocks of green as early as January sometimes.

"It was a bit of a rough winter," Hua replied, also pausing to enjoy the fresh late April weather.

Sarah knew that Hua was not just referring to the

cold and weather, but also to the evil that had threatened to topple Witchland last November—Madras Spellwood, Sarah's ancestor and sister to the powerful witch Lativia. Madras had turned to dark magic while alive, and now her evil ghost kept threatening to take over the forest and town of Witchland, both of which Lativia protected.

Sarah's golden collie mix and familiar, Addie, could tell Sarah was thinking of Madras. She looked at Sarah mournfully and barked, wagging her tail in sympathy.

"It sure was," Sarah agreed with a shudder. "I'm incredibly happy Madras is gone for good. It seems everyone wants to take over this bit of paradise, but we have a great little army."

"We sure do." Hua winked. The army Sarah was referring to was composed of local witches, of which Sarah was one.

A familiar cackle brought Sarah abruptly out of her reflections on the past November. "That one is crooked!" Harriet taunted from across the street, where she was walking by with her crow, Edgar, perched on her shoulder.

Sarah rolled her eyes and surveyed the flyer. It looked perfectly straight. She realized that Harriet was only taunting her.

"Can't see through all that mascara, huh?" Harriet continued to cackle as she walked away.

"I'm not even wearing makeup!" Sarah shouted after her.

"Don't let her bother you. She likes you; that's why she teases you." Hua laughed.

"No time to waste with banter!" Harriet shouted back without looking behind her. "I have lost my lucky bauble, and I won't be right until I find it!"

"Lucky bauble?" Sarah shook her head, watching Harriet's receding back. Then she surveyed the flyers she held in her hand. They urged people to attend the mayoral debate at the town hall tomorrow, part of the election process to replace the former mayor, who was now in prison for murdering the town clerk and stealing the town deed, which had held Lativia's protective spell against Madras. It had taken the town government some time to recover from Mayor Lewis's theft and arrest, and its acting mayor, Susan Lake, had decided that she did not want to become the official mayor. As a result, elections for a new mayor were just now taking place. "I printed four hundred on recycled paper, and so far we've put up eighty. Think we've put up enough?"

"Of course! I can't imagine anyone in this town doesn't know I'm running yet, after how hard we've campaigned," Hua said. Then she sighed. "Let's go back to my house and take a break."

Sarah followed Hua back to her lovely house, which was surrounded by gorgeous gardens just beginning to sprout. In the back, a barn converted into a greenhouse stood, and Sarah knew it was brimming with verdant plants inside. The sweet odor of churned manure with newspaper and composted food waste hovered over the place, mingling with the sharp scent of the chilly air and Margaret and Hua's woodstove smoke billowing from their chimney. This place always felt like home to Sarah, as much as her own home and the coffee shop in town where she spent a lot of her time.

Hua sighed, lowering herself into a rocker. She was neither old nor overweight, but a certain exhaustion had begun to overtake her lately. "I really just can't wait for all of this to be over, honestly." She groaned, rubbing her eyes. "Too much work! Too many meetings! And all of the planning! Now we just walked all over town and put up eighty flyers."

"There are still three hundred and twenty left." Sarah laughed. "Maybe I printed too many."

"Maybe?" Margaret teased, entering the covered porch. "I know you're exhausted, honey," she went on, handing her wife a steaming mug of fragrant tea. "This is a tea to revitalize you."

Hua beamed and puckered her lips at Margaret in a kissing gesture. "I couldn't have made it this far without you. And you," she added, including Sarah with a glance. "I think I would be in the hospital with a heart attack by now otherwise."

"All this work will be worth it in the end," Sarah reassured Hua.

"Speaking of worth it, I have to show you a new plant I acquired. It cost us an arm and a leg to order it through a seller online, but it was definitely worth it." Hua's eyes lit up the way they always did when she spoke about her two deepest passions: agronomy and plant magic. "Let's go back to the greenhouse."

"You're in for a real treat!" Margaret declared, rubbing her hands together with excitement.

Sarah followed the two herbal witches into their packed, humid greenhouse. She always wondered how the women could find specific plants among the seemingly countless species packed onto the tables and shelves, growing every which way, even through the winter.

"This baby is the Echinoflava interrupta," Hua said proudly, holding up the pot of a small, red prickly-looking plant with a single yellow flower sprouting on top.

"What does it do?" Sarah asked.

"Do you have your cell phone on you?" Margaret

asked. She was beaming, as was Hua; the two clearly anticipated that Sarah would be stunned by whatever the plant could do to her phone.

Sarah produced her phone from her back pocket.

"Hold it up to the plant. See what happens," Hua urged.

Sarah did as she was instructed. Instantly, her screen went fuzzy and then black. She tried to turn it back on, but it would not work. "Oh, no," she cried in dismay.

"Now go stand a few feet away," Hua instructed.

Sarah hurried away from the plant and breathed in relief as her phone finally turned back on. She had too many important contacts and pictures on that phone to lose it all to some electronic-interfering plant.

"It blocks all electronics! Literally scrambles their electromagnetic energy so that they can't work!" Margaret crowed.

Hua clapped her hands exuberantly. "And this baby . . ." She led Sarah on to another strange-looking dark fern. "This one is like a catnip for foxes. As you know, we are going through a period where our foxes are dying because of distemper introduced by feral dogs, and this plant could help."

"We should plant it everywhere," Sarah exclaimed.

"Not so fast. We have to test it first, to make sure it

won't disrupt the ecosystem here," Margaret informed her.

"Now take this plant, for instance. This one is drawn to metal," Margaret went on, leading Sarah deeper into the greenery of the building. She showed how the vines of the plant curled desperately, almost greedily, around a metal stake. Then she held a penny up to the plant. Rapidly, a leaf unfurled, grew toward the penny, curled around it, and then snatched it and retreated to hold the coin close to its stem.

"We call it the greedy morning glory," Hua announced. "Very rare, from the Japanese island of Kyushu. People there think it's evil and try to eradicate it."

"Another part of our job as witches is keeping these species alive, ensuring they are not destroyed," Margaret added.

Sarah gently touched the leaves of the plant and felt a vague, warm energy emanating from it. "Yeah, it's not a bad-spirited plant," she agreed. She knew what bad spirits felt like now, quite well.

"I want to try something with you. I want you to tell me what a plant can do by scanning it," Hua declared.

Sarah thought of Michael Howler in his wolf form, still eager to help her communicate with ghosts, plants, and animals. Michael had been her mentor in law school and after she landed her first job at a real estate law firm; however, she had had no idea he was a powerful warlock until she moved to Witchland and spoke to his ghost atop Mount Katribus. Now he was also her mentor in magic, just as the other witches in Witchland were. After she had inherited his law practice in Witchland, where he had spent his last years, she had solved his murder and put his killer behind bars for life. Now she took care of his dog, Addie, and continued his work advocating for the protection of the Witchland Forest from human activities, such as development and poaching. No matter what, she was not alone.

"Um, how do I begin?" she asked, as Hua and Margaret led her to a nondescript, nonflowering plant growing near their robust, colorful tomatoes.

"First, clear your mind," Hua instructed her.

Sarah began to clear her mind, a difficult task that she had become increasingly good at.

"Now, reach out to the plant. It can be helpful to envision your mind as a hand. When you touch the plant, you will feel him touch you back, and then he will speak to you," Margaret went on.

After a few frustrating failures, Sarah started to imagine the strange day in the forest when she had first heard Addie speak. She vividly remembered her shock, and her fear that she was losing her mind. Then she remembered how she came to know Addie as a sentient being with a voice. It turned out that all beings had such a voice and full consciousness, far more than most people guessed. This plant had a mind and spirit and, thus, something to say. Focusing on that knowledge, she felt herself start to stretch beyond her frame, out of her skin. She felt herself brush against the plant, even though she was not physically touching it.

Only then did her mind fill with a pleasant, clear male voice with a cadence much like a wind chime. *"Hello there,"* it said.

Sarah took a startled step backward. *"Why, hello,"* she replied, glancing at her mentors, who were smiling.

"I'm Nipkin," the plant said.

"I'm Sarah. Pleased to meet you. What do you . . . do, Nipkin?" she asked.

"What do I do?" He paused. Before Sarah could clarify what she had meant, he began to sing, *"I grow tall and lean! And the sun shines down on me, down on me. The birds peck at me, oh, they peck at me, and I know I'll be back in spring. From a little seed, a little seed, I spring, and the caterpillars inch along me!"*

"Do you feed the birds?" Sarah inquired. *"That's your purpose, feeding birds?"*

"And caterpillars and worms and things! I feed, I feed, I feed. Things grow from me." Nipkin seemed quite content with himself as Sarah thanked him for

speaking with her. *"Oh, of course!"* he sang. *"I like speaking to things, to the living beings, to the things that feed on me, on me."*

"I suppose he's . . . he's a food plant?" Sarah told Hua and Margaret, unsure how to clearly describe what Nipkin had just told her about himself.

"He is a type of milkweed that is almost extinct due to a nearly complete loss of habitat. He is very critical to his ecosystem," Margaret said proudly. "Even the simplest plants matter immensely in the big picture."

Sarah glanced back at Nipkin, his sweet spirit tugging at her heartstrings. She felt a tear form in her eye.

Hua and Margaret clapped their hands, beaming. "That is today's lesson!" Hua declared, pleased with Sarah's pupilage.

"Do you want to come over for a home-cooked dinner?" Sarah texted Eli as she walked back to her cottage, Addie prancing along at her side. Sarah felt butterflies fluttering in her gut every time she was near him and even when she texted him. Focusing on her phone, she nearly walked into a light pole. She cried out, and Addie barked, *"Sarah, are you okay?"*

"I'm fine. Nothing hurt but my pride." Sarah glanced around, hoping that Harriet was not observing her. Relieved to not see the hunchbacked witch in her pointy hat, Sarah stooped to pick up some of the vegetables she had spilled from the large basket she carried of produce that Hua and Margaret had helped her harvest from their greenhouse. They had been teaching her how to ask plants for permission before picking their fruits or flowers. Sarah found it endearing how eager plants were to give of themselves in order to promote life elsewhere. It reminded her of the plant who had launched itself out of its pot and smashed into Dismas's head in the doctor's office, when her rival, John Gonforth, and his henchman, Dismas Lorian, held her hostage with every intention of killing her. Repotting the plant had saved its life, but it had been willing to die for her.

"You need to watch where you're going and not get all flustered over Eli," Addie teased.

"I can't help it." Sarah laughed, her cheeks turning rosy pink. Then she blushed even harder when her phone dinged and she saw Eli's name on the screen. *"This guy makes me feel like a high school girl with her first crush."*

"Oh, for dog biscuits' sake," Addie teased.

"Home-cooked? I can just pick up something from Geno's," Eli replied.

"We've been eating out way too much. I can already feel myself gaining a little pooch," Sarah replied. "Let's eat something healthy at home, my treat."

"For sure! I've never tried your cooking. Can't wait. Be there in a few," he texted back.

Sarah beamed as she unlocked the front door. Most people did not lock their doors in Witchland, but Sarah did it faithfully, every time she went out. Though Witchland was the most peaceful place she had ever lived, she had survived her first break-in the year before, as she battled against John Gonforth and his developer goons, who had desired rights to demolish the forest and build a series of hotels and shopping centers in its place. Besides, she was from New York, and a New Yorker is always a New Yorker at heart.

Which was also why her heart always nearly stopped when Kelvin trotted up to the door. "Oh, Kelvin, I wasn't expecting you," she said.

"*I let myself in through the window,*" he replied casually as he licked Addie hello.

"How on earth did you do that?" Sarah asked.

"*Easy. I opened the latch with my teeth,*" he replied.

Kelvin was a wolf that Sarah and Addie had found in the woods last fall. He often paid Addie visits and stayed the night in Sarah's home, much like a regular dog. At first, it had made Sarah nervous to be near such a wild animal, whose overwhelming power was apparent in his sinewy muscle and powerful jaws. But she knew he did not intend to hurt her—or any humans, for that matter—and his love for Addie eclipsed his desire to hunt in town. To protect him from neighbors who might not take so kindly to his presence, Sarah cloaked him in a camouflaging spell she herself had used to defeat Madras last fall. She renewed the spell every morning. While it kept Kelvin invisible to animal control officers and hunters who might cause him harm, especially within the village limits, it also allowed both Sarah and Addie to see him. Kelvin appreciated the spell because it made hunting in the woods even easier and it meant he could see his girlfriend whenever he pleased.

"Tell me, what's the plan?" Addie asked, her chops already watering in anticipation of the aromas soon to fill the house.

"Chicken, I hope," Kelvin said, his chops also watering.

"I want to surprise Eli with some stir fry," Sarah replied. "I picked up tofu at the market the other day." She began rummaging in the fridge for fresh ingredients.

Addie looked displeased. *"What on earth is tofu?"*

Sarah sighed. The one thing she and Addie could never agree on was eating meat. Sarah always made fresh chicken and trout for Addie's special home-cooked food, which Addie now shared with Kelvin, but Sarah refused to let meat pass through her own lips, not even fish. Since she was a little girl, eating meat always made her feel intensely depressed. Only now did she understand it was because she had a close intuitive connection with animals that had been passed down through many generations of the Spellwood family. When she ate meat, she could feel the pain and fear the animals had experienced as they died.

"I'm just glad Eli is starting to come around to veganism, too," she muttered. "Since you two never will." She shot Addie and Kelvin a teasing look.

"Yeah, good luck making me eat that." Kelvin wrinkled his nose when he smelled the tofu as Sarah removed it from its package. *"Gross!"*

"Go eat your own food! You know you don't get table scraps!" Sarah responded.

"He doesn't, but I sneak some when you're not looking," Addie quipped as she trotted to her bed near the kitchen entrance.

Kelvin followed her and sat near her as she laid down. He always had to be close to her, which melted Sarah's heart.

"Hello!" Eli called, stepping into the doorway.

"Back here, love!" Sarah answered.

Eli entered the kitchen and planted a firm kiss on

her cheek. Then he sat at the tiny table. "I have a little bit of paperwork to finish up, but I wanted to come by, in case you needed any help."

"Nope! I got it!" she said cheerfully as she commenced chopping vegetables. "Soooo, how was your day?"

Eli told her about the events in great detail as he watched her, the smile on his face tight. Suddenly, he shouted, "Sarah!"

Sarah froze and looked down. The knife was mere micromillimeters from her fingertip. "Wow, that would've been bad." She giggled with embarrassment.

"Um, do you want me to chop the veggies?" he asked.

"No, no, I got it." She waved him away. "This is my night to cook for you!"

"It's just . . . I've never seen someone handle a knife like that," he went on. He then chuckled nervously. "Have you ever even chopped vegetables before?"

"*She doesn't have much practice,*" Addie spoke up.

"*Quiet, Addie.*" Sarah groaned. "I'm fine. I got this."

"All right then." Eli held his hands up and went back to his paperwork.

Sarah fetched an egg and went to crack it as an extra treat for Kelvin and Addie. She realized she didn't have a spatula, so she set the egg on the countertop. It promptly began to roll off the counter. Kelvin dashed into the kitchen and caught it on the tip of his nose, balancing it for Sarah to retrieve.

"Geez, this must be my lucky day." Sarah laughed.

"Are you using magic?" Eli inquired, watching her closely. Since moving to Witchland from Buffalo, where he had worked as a cop and grown up in a law family, he had slowly come to accept that magic was real and that it abounded in Witchland. Dating a witch had never been part of his life's plan, and he still seemed uncertain talking about Sarah's abilities, but he supported her wholeheartedly in her magical training.

"No! Though I probably could." Sarah beamed as she began to regale Eli with all of her newly acquired expertise on the subject.

Eli smiled, showing appropriate interest, though most of what she told him went over his head. "I'm surprised you're spending so much time on plants. Didn't Lativia Spellwood tell you to focus more on other types of magic?" he finally said when she finished relating her lessons for the day with Hua and Margaret.

Sarah paused. Eli had a great point. "I don't really know where to start with all of that," she admitted finally. "All of the witches here and the Leekins use plant and herbal magic. And Lativia's spellbook only seems to work when I need it to. Usually, it is far too complicated for me to use."

"Why don't you start with some books written by other witches? I saw one the other day in the library about animal spirit guides," Eli suggested. "You know, since you're so close to animals and can commune with them, wouldn't that be a great starting point for animal magic?"

"That's a good idea, but I'm incredibly overwhelmed and busy right now as it is, studying environmental law and herbalism. I can't chug through another dense book," Sarah responded. She made a mental note to look into the book and ask Hua and Margaret about animal spirit guides at some point because she knew it was a good idea.

"You always underestimate yourself," Eli said, coming up behind her and wrapping his strong arms around her waist. His proximity and manly scent always made her feel as if she could swoon, like in some 1950s romance. "If only you saw the powerful, badass witch I see," he added, nibbling her earlobe.

CHAPTER TWO

SARAH HELD ELI'S HAND WHILE THEY SCANNED for empty seats in the town square, which had been filled with neat rows of folding chairs facing a makeshift stage with a beribboned podium set upon it.

Jenna Mora, Eli's deputy, grinned and waved them over to the two seats she had reserved for them in the front row, right by Hua and Margaret. She was wearing regular clothes, which threw Sarah off; Sarah had never seen Jenna in anything other than her crisp, blue cop uniform. Jenna's smoky eye makeup was also a surprise. Sarah briefly wondered if Jenna was still into Eli; Jenna had once had a thing for her cop partner, but had conceded him to Sarah after realizing how he felt for Sarah. The jealousy that had once lingered between them like a vague, sour cloud had dissipated over time. Jenna's huge grin seemed to be proof of that.

As they made their way to the seats Jenna had saved them, an elderly lady stopped them. "You finally found someone!" she crowed to Eli, beaming.

Eli smiled, looking awkward. "This is Sarah Spellwood."

"Oh, I know who you are! So pretty!" The lady pinched Sarah's cheek as if she were ten years old. "When is the wedding?" she added.

Eli and Sarah exchanged awkward glances. "We haven't quite gotten there yet. We're still getting to know each other," Eli finally answered.

"You had better get to it! The clock is ticking!" the woman said.

"No boundaries," Sarah said with a laugh when the lady had shuffled out of earshot.

Eli sighed. "Old Mrs. Marple means well, but yes, she has no boundaries. Geez, I still can't get used to how everyone knows everyone's business in this town!"

"Me neither. In some ways, it's very nice, but the anonymity of the big city does have its perks," Sarah agreed.

Now that they had been dating for a few months, people had finally stopped staring and telling them how cute they were—for the most part. Sarah had not realized how many old women in town wanted to fix Eli up with someone, and they found Sarah to be the answer to their prayers and years of effort. While it was cute, it could get a bit annoying at times as well. In a town as small as Witchland, nobody had secrets for long, and privacy was practically nonexistent. News of their relationship had spread like wildfire, and now everyone knew the details of Sarah's love life.

After saying hello to some more people, Eli and Sarah sat in the chairs next to Jenna. Sarah still held his hand, and loved how unwilling he was to let go. *Jeff never held my hand like this in public*, she thought, a smile tugging at her lips. *I never thought during my divorce that I would ever be happy again, but I am even happier actually! I sure got lucky. Some things are just blessings in disguise.*

Sarah scanned the crowd. Almost everyone in Witchland was present. She always loved how events like this brought everyone together, catching up and warmly greeting each other. People never greeted others in the crowds of New York; but here, people cared about one another and maintained tight friend-ships. Even enemies were more like "frenemies," talking often and taking comfort from the familiarity of their rivalry. It was heartwarming. Sarah sensed that in Witchland, she would never, ever be alone. It was a nice feeling, compared to the bleakness she felt in New York City after her husband Jeff had left her and her job had turned sour.

The town's director of administration and stand-in

mayor, Susan Lake, stepped out onto the little stage and welcomed everyone to the mayoral debate. "As we all know, our history with mayors . . . turned dark last fall," Susan began somberly. "Witchland deserves better. While I have enjoyed acting as mayor during the election, I must say that I am old and very tired."

Polite laughter rippled through the crowd.

"Therefore, I am eager to hand over the reins to the most qualified candidate, and we are all here today to help determine who that candidate is! We are here to usher in a more positive term with a new candidate, a breath of fresh air in our town, if you will! Now let's hear it for our first speaker, Roger Miller." Susan stepped aside, and people clapped as Roger Miller stood and clambered up to the podium.

A small man with a rather undignified comb-over, Roger clutched the microphone and began to speak hurriedly, spittle flying from his mouth in his nervous state. "I just want to start by saying that I love Witchland. I grew up here, moved away for college, and couldn't stay gone for long. I knew this was where I wanted to raise my family. I hurried back as soon as I could." He paused to breathe; it was clear public speaking was not his forte. "Anyway, um, I love Witchland. So how could, um, I change it? My goal as mayor is to, um, not change anything. Anything at all."

The audience remained silent, appraising the trembling, sweating man before them. Roger watched them for a second, clearly expecting a response, before launching into more of his speech.

"I guess that sounds bad. I don't mean it to. I mean, I don't want to sound like I'm not going to do *anything* as mayor! I, um, have some plans," he rushed on.

"Like?" Daisy spoke up. She sat a few rows back from Sarah. When Sarah glanced at her and smiled, she winked back. Her dreads were now tipped in purple.

"Like maybe acquiring more land to add to our forest. You know, hiking, fishing, hunting grounds. Preserved habitat. We can have Youth Conservation Corps come in and expand our trails. Maybe add, um, another campground." His hands shaking, he removed a folded map from his pocket. He held it up, and only a few people in the front row could see where he had circled a vast area in red pen. "This is the territory I wish to acquire, actually. Just on the other side of Mount Katribus. Adding this land will greatly boost our land value, our value as a town . . . tourism . . . and general recreation."

People began to murmur to each other and nod. The general mood felt approving. But then Susan Lake spoke up, "That's a great idea, Roger, but where do you plan to get the funds for this? We're not exactly a rich municipality, you know."

"Yeah! We've been asking for you guys to fix the potholes in front of the school for two years now!" someone shouted from the back of the crowd.

"And what about the roof over the library? It's showing signs of water damage, and you know what will happen to the books when it leaks all the way through!" the town librarian added worriedly while wringing her hands.

Roger stammered and shifted his weight from one foot to the other. "Uh . . . we'll have to do a fundraiser? Maybe a bake sale or something?"

His reply was met with silence, then someone laughed and said, "A bake sale? This isn't raising money for a girls' volleyball trip, Roger; it's raising serious money!"

The audience started to pelt him with questions about funding and other town issues for another ten minutes. Roger did not seem to have any answers. He gradually turned redder and redder and shook more and more.

"I feel kind of sorry for him," Sarah muttered to Eli, her cheeks flushing in empathetic embarrassment.

Eli nodded and shrugged.

Finally, Susan Lake stepped onto the podium and thanked Roger, shaking his hand. He hastily returned to his seat, appearing defeated. Sarah watched how his shoulders stayed slumped for the remainder of the debate.

"I like his idea, but I wish he had some more solidity to his plan," a ghostly voice whispered behind Sarah. Sarah felt goosebumps and realized that Michael had joined her. Since his death, Sarah sometimes communed with him in his ghostly form on the summit of Mount Katribus, where all of Witchland's ghosts congregated to commune with the living who knew where to find them. Sarah also often visited his grave in the forest. But now she had started to see him regularly, since she had been honing her gifts. Of course, he would attend this event; he cared deeply about the fate of Witchland and its surrounding woodlands.

Telepathically, Sarah responded to Michael, "*I agree. I'd love to see more woodland belonging to Witchland itself! Since the federal government and the state can't be trusted to preserve their forests, maybe the town government can do a better job.*"

The next candidate to speak was Malorie Vulpes. She was a small, short woman, but she possessed a large presence, and she was hard to miss with her fiery red hair and the splash of freckles across her nose like cinnamon on toast. Though personable and friendly, her eyes always had a certain twinkle in them, like she was two steps ahead of everyone else. She was easily one of the most profitable business owners in the town, despite being no older than thirty. Sarah had not had much time to get to know Malorie, but now she found her curiosity about the woman piqued. She hadn't even known Malorie was running.

"As you all know," she began her speech in a strong voice, "I moved to Witchland about two years ago. Now, you all are probably wondering why you would vote for someone so new to the town. You should because I can make this town money. I converted a Victorian mansion into the Witchland Bed and Breakfast, and I operate several Airbnbs in the town. I am a small business owner—and proud of it. My goal is to support businesses in this town and bring in more.

"I hear you all," Malorie went on. "Witchland is wonderful, and none of us want this town to change . . . too much. But we also have a budget problem, a big one, actually. Previous attempts to take over this town and turn it into a tourism mecca of high-rise hotels and chain restaurants have failed, and rightly so. That's not what I'm proposing. But I think our future rides on tourism. I mean, look at this place!" She spread her arms out wide, indicating the flourishing trees, growing flowers, and charming, quaint buildings surrounding the square, with Mount Katribus looming verdantly in the background.

Two different energies immediately seized the

crowd. A few business owners nodded and cheered in agreement, as did the librarian and the gentleman concerned about the potholes. But another woman stood and shouted, "I don't want my town overtaken by people I don't know! That brings crime and prostitution and drugs and all sorts of things!" Several people echoed her sentiments.

Malorie nodded thoughtfully. "That is a valid concern, yes. But I was prepared for such a concern. I already looked into crime stats at other tourist towns. Salem, for example. Salem is also based on magical tourism, and it has a lower crime rate than we do, actually! There is no higher crime rate in tourism towns than in towns with lower tourist rates."

"How do you propose to bring in more tourism?" Susan Lake questioned.

Malorie grinned, her passion and intelligence once again flashing in her eyes. "We have to give the tourists something to do. Hiking Mount Katribus is not enough. First, we advertise the camping more, and we fix up our campground. A witch theme, a clubhouse with a pool table and foosball. We bring in more restaurants—Chinese, a traditional crab shack with some great clam chowder, another bakery or two. Next, we build a bar, with a New England witch theme. People will eat that up. Feature bands and dancing at night, like a nightclub! I have already looked into the alcohol permit and business license we need for such a place."

Several residents cried out in dismay. "I don't mind wine at Geno's, but a full-service liquor bar? You'll get all sorts of lechers in here, bar fights, and all of that!" an older gentleman shouted in distress.

"And floozies in short skirts!" his shrewish wife shouted.

"The last thing we want to do is pollute our town with those kinds of people—and those values. We are a pure town," the librarian spoke up.

"But think of the jobs it'll bring! Kids saving up for college could really use the tips and the experience," Malorie urged.

The crowd dissolved into argument, with two opposing factions arguing for and against Malorie. It was clear that she had struck a nerve with some people. Sarah was disturbed to see Eli nodding and grinning, clearly enamored with her plan.

"You don't really support all of this, do you?" she whispered.

"Why not? It's a brilliant idea. Bring some more cash in. Fix up the town. The people would certainly benefit. And it's not like she's calling for the destruction of our forest—she's actually planning to use it for something beneficial to us all," he responded.

"But I hate to see Witchland change at all," Sarah

replied, her heart sinking. She and Eli had never had a difference in opinion before. "I love this place. She is planning to change its spirit. That is just not right."

Eli sighed. "It's really not as big of a deal as people are making it out to be. It's not like she's proposing a strip club. She just wants to open a little place where people can have a few cocktails and some wings. And think about it, wouldn't it be fun to go out Friday nights and dance?" He affectionately pinched her arm.

It was true. Though she and Eli spent a lot of time in the woods and at Javacadabra, the local coffee shop, they did not have a wide variety of options for their date nights. They usually just ate out and then watched movies at Sarah's house, on Michael's tiny, grainy television. Eli always complained that he had to rent VHS because Michael's TV was too old to support an HDMI cable. Sometimes they went to Eli's, which was even more cramped and uncomfortable, being a classic bachelor pad with sparse décor, a tiny futon couch, and only a hard twin mattress. Eli didn't even have proper plates; he used paper, saying he didn't have time for dishes. But Sarah didn't mind traveling to other bigger towns farther away for nightlife. Why did they need to change Witchland just to have more interesting dates? She was about to argue with Eli some more when Susan announced the final candidate.

Hua climbed onto the stage. Sarah, Eli, Margaret,

and Jenna all cheered. Hua grinned, trying not to betray her nerves as she assembled her notes on the podium before her. "Hello, everyone. As you all know, I'm a gardener, by trade and by heart. My wife, Margaret, and I used to live in Manhattan. We came here for peace and quiet, and that's what we got. But we also got more than that." She paused, taking in the crowd before her. "We got a loving home. We got family, who accepted us with their arms wide open. Because of the people of Witchland, because of all you have given us, we want to give you something back. That's why I'm running for mayor."

A few people clapped or called out how much they loved Margaret and Hua. But then Susan Lake spoke, "What are you hoping to accomplish with your office, Hua?"

Hua paused, racing over her notes. "More town gardens. An after-school program to help kids learn to garden. A witch museum, to showcase the history of this town and honor its roots with Lativia Spellwood. And, of course, a mass volunteer effort and lobbying for state help to fix our roads and our library."

People nodded, and a few more clapped. After all, it was clear she had the good of the town at heart, and the most practical, nonradical ideas for how to achieve that goal. Sarah wondered if she should vote for her, not just because she was a dear friend but because she seemed like the most even-keeled candidate. At the same time, she did like Roger's plan.

"Not everyone is that into gardening," the shrewish woman spoke out. "Kids who want to garden should learn that at home, not at school."

"What good would more gardens do us, anyway? Every spare inch of this town is cloaked in garden," yet another person spoke up.

"You know the state doesn't care about us," another person objected. "How on earth do you expect them to care about our library and our roads?"

"And these are municipal issues, anyway," yet another person challenged. "Not state. They won't help us. What we need is a way to generate more municipal tax revenue. There isn't a high enough population or enough industry to pay for all the town's needs as it is. Malorie has the right ideas!"

"Malorie for mayor!" the grocer shouted, sticking his fist into the air.

Hua looked increasingly deflated and flustered as she attempted to answer the challenges and questions flung at her. Soon, people were shouting at each other over her, completely drowning out her voice.

The applause and questions finally died down. Susan Lake thanked everyone for coming and urged them to vote in the ballots next week. The audience then promptly began to split apart into little groups of people locked in fervent political discussion.

Hua joined Margaret, who bear-hugged her and assured her she had done well. Sarah jogged up to Hua and patted her on the back. "That was tough, but you really held your own."

"I guess we'll just have to see the polling results," Hua replied sadly. "I really wanted to do my part here. I didn't realize it would be so tough today."

"You still do a huge part in this community!" Eli told her.

"I'll have to see you guys later," Jenna said as her radio became suddenly active with some dispatch chatter about a cat in a tree again. "Duty calls."

"I'm not taking that call," Eli told her with exasperation. "I have gotten Finkles out of that spruce tree ten times this month."

Jenna laughed. "It's fine. I'll have one of the other deputies do it this time. You two enjoy yourselves." She hurried away, answering the dispatch.

"See? That's why we love it here. Albeit there have been two horrible murders, usually that's the worst of the crime." Hua sighed.

"It gets boring at times," Eli admitted, "but I far prefer it to Buffalo!"

"Hey guys, we had better go tend to the plants," Margaret said, excusing herself and Hua. After Eli and

Sarah said goodbye, the two witches headed away, Hua still looking slightly upset.

"I really liked Roger's message, honestly," Sarah began. "I know I should vote for Hua, but I love the idea of protecting more woodland."

Eli sighed. "I do, too, babe. But where will we get the money? Our town is broke, Sarah."

"Where there's a will, there's a way," Sarah replied. She firmly believed it, too. In the past, whenever she had encountered an insurmountable challenge, she found that perseverance and faith in herself always brought about great results.

He sighed again. "The Leekins aren't going to be able to raise the money this time."

Sarah prickled. "What's that supposed to mean? That I can only do things with the Leekins' help?" She pulled away from Eli, incensed at this patronizing side of him. She had glimpsed it once or twice before, but it had never rankled her as much as now.

Eli placed a firm, reassuring hand on Sarah's shoulder. "Don't take what I said the wrong way. I didn't mean any offense. I was just saying there is a line between the material world and the magical world, and it doesn't always blur. There may be a will and a way or whatever with magic, but not always with money. The money has to come from somewhere. It definitely doesn't grow on trees!"

I bet Hua and Margaret have a money tree, Sarah thought with a smirk. But she didn't say that out loud. Instead, she said firmly, "I just don't think Malorie's idea is a good one." She had never been one to give up on voicing her opinions. "I just don't want to see Witchland change into something it's not. I think we can find another way to raise the money and make Roger's plan happen."

"You're being naïve," he said, a slight tinge of annoyance in his voice.

Feeling patronized, Sarah bristled. Then she decided to let it go. This was a small tiff. She didn't like the way Eli called her naïve, but she also knew he never meant any harm with anything he did or said. She had to remind herself that he was nothing like her ex-husband, who had always been highly critical and haughty.

CHAPTER THREE

Sarah, Addie, and Eli followed Susie and Karen, the owners of Javacadabra, back to the café for lunch. Addie laid down on Sarah's feet after giving her customary bark to Zeva, the shop's patron white cat, who ignored her as usual.

"Some debate that was, huh?" Susie remarked as she began to set up her espresso machine.

"I really don't want to even talk about it," Karen responded, her voice full of stress. She retired to the back to start cooking Sarah's and Eli's orders, as well as a treat for Addie. She used to be opposed to having pets besides Zeva in her coffee shop due to health codes, but she had slowly come around to Susie's habit of letting people bring their pets inside. Begrudgingly, she admitted that Addie was her favorite patron of all, and she betrayed her inner softness for animals by often making Addie a special something to go along with Sarah's meals. Nevertheless, she and Susie often proved the point that opposites attract. Sarah got the sense that they had disagreed about who was the best candidate, as well.

Though they no longer discussed the political issue now dividing the town as they ate, Sarah had the sense that Eli was far away mentally. "What are you thinking about?" she finally asked.

"Another place for lunch," he responded with a little laugh. "Aren't you tired of the same things every day? They only have a few vegan options."

"I guess I'm used to it," Sarah replied, staring down at her plate, her appetite gone. "Most restaurants don't carry much that is vegan, if anything at all."

"I bet you miss that about New York," Eli went on. "All of the food options and vegan places to eat."

"I miss nothing about New York," she answered honestly.

As she walked home after lunch with Addie, she felt a bit stunned and rankled. She never imagined that Eli might see things differently than she did, but of course he would. After all, he was his own person. A relationship didn't mean that they saw eye to eye on *everything*, right?

"I just felt he was being cluelessly patronizing. I don't like Malorie's proposal, sorry," she told Addie, her number-one confidante.

"*She's not what she seems to be,*" Addie said slowly.

"What do you mean by that?" Sarah inquired. She always paid attention to things Addie said. Addie had a very sharp instinct, especially about people. In many ways, she was more intuitive than Sarah was, and thus, she and Sarah made a solid team.

"*Something about her scent is off,*" Addie said, shaking her head. "*I can't place it. It's . . . wild. Odd. Not quite human.*"

Sarah froze. "Are you saying she's not human?"

"*No, not necessarily. I don't know. She might be a shapeshifter,*" Addie mused.

"Michael is a shapeshifter. What did he smell like?" Sarah prodded.

"*Nothing like her, but that's because he's a wolf,*" was all Addie could say.

"Michael, are you still there?" Sarah called.

Michael soon answered. "I sense I'm needed?" His voice sounded far off, and Sarah realized he was probably tired, eager to return to the woods for rest. Ghosts needed rest much more than the living.

"Do you think there's something off about Malorie?" she asked. "Could she be an animal shapeshifter, like you?"

"Something I can't place. She doesn't want me to see her clearly," Michael answered vaguely. When he got tired, his answers became vague and more spacey.

Sarah shook her head. "I don't like this at all. She never struck me as evil."

"She's not evil," Michael affirmed. "Just . . . different. I can't place it. Anyway, it's time for my nap. Good afternoon!"

As they returned to Michael's house, Sarah found herself lost in thought. Suddenly, Addie took off, the way she did when she caught a scent trail too juicy to ignore. "Addie! Wait!" Sarah cried, startled out of her reverie as Addie crashed through the bushes with her nose plastered to the ground. She chased Addie around to the side of the house.

She found Addie wagging her tail with her snorting snout buried into a bush. "What is it, girl?" Sarah asked, dropping to her knees and peering through the tangled branches of the evergreen shrub to see what Addie was after. Though she couldn't quite tell what it was, it looked like a small piece of paper, or some type of card.

"Grab it! It's for you!" Addie prompted Sarah.

Confused, Sarah cautiously reached through the

scraggly branches and closed her fingers around the card. It felt like a big playing card of some type. She pulled it out and flipped it over to see a picture of a handsome lynx posed against a forest backdrop.

"What's this? It's beautiful." She turned the card around to survey its back more closely. The card seemed new and was printed on stiff cardstock.

"*It's a lynx,*" Addie said matter-of-factly.

"I can see that. But what *is* it?" Sarah mused. "Some type of tarot card?"

Addie took off again. "*I smell another one!*" Not far from the lynx card, she located another, this one depicting a wolf. The wolf looked like Kelvin, and Addie sighed longingly looking at it.

"You're so silly." Sarah rolled her eyes lovingly. Addie's little love affair with the wolf from the woods still tickled her. She turned the new card over in her hands, now truly perplexed. Was it a coincidence that her spirit guide was a wolf?

Then Sarah spotted another in some grass. It was a crow, shiny and black, perched on an oak tree branch.

Addie finally retrieved the fourth card from another nearby bush, bringing it to Sarah in her mouth. As Sarah wiped Addie's saliva off of the card on her pant leg, she flipped it over and saw something that made her freeze.

The card showed a fox, bushy and red and white.

"I think we might need to investigate this some more," she told Addie. "Someone put these here intentionally. Why else would they be littered around my house?"

"It's some message, and they smell off," Addie told her. *"Like a human, but not quite. Maybe someone who sleeps in the woods?"*

"Like a transient?" Sarah asked.

"I don't know. Someone did place them here, not too long ago. Maybe an hour ago?"

"That's mysterious. And there are no other cards?" Sarah inquired, glancing around the little space behind Michael's house.

"Not that I can tell. And you know *how sharp my nose is."*

Sarah put the four cards in her pocket. "I might have to ask Hua and Margaret about these. Or Daisy. I sense they have some kind of deeper meaning. Let's go study, girl." She led Addie inside to resume her fervent study of environmental and paranormal law. She often read late into the nights when Eli didn't come over.

In the morning, Sarah thought over what she had to do for the day. Her caseload was very light at the moment, leaving her with just hefting heavy law books onto her desk to pore over until she couldn't absorb another fact. She decided she needed a break from that today, after studying until two a.m. the night before, so she asked Addie to accompany her to the area of forest Roger wanted to acquire for the town.

"*Yay! Hike!*" Addie shouted ecstatically, jumping up and twirling around on her back legs.

The patch of forest lay on the other side of Mount Katribus, where the Leekins lived. It was outside of the Witchland State Forest. After cresting the mountain peak, Sarah found herself overlooking a pristine expanse of rich, green forest, with a few stark-naked trees still not bathed in buds yet. The birds twittered from below, and the scent of rich, mossy earth protected from sunlight and humans tickled her nostrils. A broad-winged hawk soared overhead, a dark cloud of finches rising to fend him off.

"How beautiful. We really would benefit from adding this patch of forest to the Witchland Forest," she remarked out loud.

"*I would love to hike through those woods and smell all of the new scents!*" Addie sprang around, her nose quivering as she drew in countless new scents and aromas.

Sarah found a small patch of white mushrooms shooting up through the earth around a rotting tree trunk. She wondered if her experience in the greenhouse with Nipkin the Milkweed might work on mushrooms and other fungi, as well. Gently, she cleared her mind and reached out to touch the mushrooms psychically.

Quickly, she became keenly aware of an overwhelming sense of the mushroom's spirit. It seemed calm, dense, and earthy, grounding even. While it did not speak to her clearly as Nipkin had, it was certainly communicating with her, letting her know who it was. A strong but pleasant spongy scent and taste filled her throat. Suddenly, she was filled with a deep, intuitive understanding of its complex fibrous root system, the way it broke down nutrients in the earth, the way it fed the next cycle of life, the feeling of rain caressing its smooth skin. For a few moments, she enjoyed the sensation of being a mushroom.

"I wonder when I will find my other animal spirit guides," Sarah mused as she thanked the mushroom and pulled back into her normal state of being. "I really want to know what they have to tell me. Something is missing, and it is frustrating."

"I'm sure she will come to you soon," Addie assured her.

A familiar small voice interrupted their conversation, "Hey!"

Sarah and Addie turned to see the Leekins forming

a pyramid behind them, making a throne for Clover Figcreek to stand on top. Her wings trembled as she alighted on her fellow Leekins, putting her at a height where she could look Sarah in the eye.

"What brings you to this part of the woods?" Clover Figcreek inquired. Though she was only the size of a large black ant, her commanding voice filled Sarah's ears as if Clover Figcreek were a full-sized adult human. The other Leekins buzzed beneath her, their little wings beating as they stood in a perfect pyramid.

"If the town elects Roger Miller as mayor, we could acquire this part of the woods. Currently it is state property, open to hunters. We could make it a municipal park and, therefore, end hunting," Sarah said proudly.

All of the Leekins turned bright pink with pleasure and let out yips of joy. "The Blackberry Hoppers will also be pleased to hear this," Clover Figcreek announced.

Sarah smiled, recollecting the strange faeries called Blackberry Hoppers that dwelled on the mountain behind Mount Katribus. While she had never seen them, Clover Figcreek had mentioned Sarah's misadventures in the cave system under the mountains had ended a decades-long feud with the creatures. "Are the

Blackberry Hoppers starting to mingle with you on this side of the mountain?" Sarah asked.

Clover Figcreek let out a shrill whistle. A few seconds later, dozens of grasshoppers began to leap out of the grass and land around the Leekin pyramid. Upon closer inspection, Sarah realized these were not grasshoppers at all, but rather tiny faeries with powerful hind legs and lean vertical bodies, built like grasshoppers. They sported shocks of vibrantly colored hair on top of their oddly human heads, and their insect-like bodies were streaked with color as well. They had large, round, metallic insect eyes set on the sides of their long faces.

"Are you the Blackberry Hoppers?" Sarah gasped. Addie woofed, perplexed by these faery folk that she had never seen before.

"I am Lily Silverhopper," declared the largest Hopper in a ringing voice. She had a copper-colored spray of hair, green insect eyes, and a burnished silver sheen to her body. "I am the leader of the Blackberry Hoppers. Why have we been called forth?"

"I wanted you to meet Sarah Spellwood," Clover Figcreek replied, a trace of haughtiness in her voice. "She is our liaison to the human folk."

"Pleased to meet you, ancestor of Lativia Spellwood," Lily Silverhopper said with solemn deference.

The other Blackberry Hoppers behind her whirred in greeting. "Our kind knew your ancestor, and we have passed down many stories about your family over the generations. We look forward to a working relationship."

"Hey!" Clover Figcreek cried petulantly. "I said that she is *our* liaison, not yours!"

"If we want to protect the environment from human activity and evil like Madras, we must all work together," Sarah responded gently. "After all, what happens in the vicinity of Mount Katribus also affects Mount Katribus and Witchland. We're all in this together."

"Perhaps you should remind the Leekins of that fact, since they poisoned our territory with an invasive plant species," Lily Silverhopper declared.

"Are you still on about that?" Clover Figcreek said exasperatedly. "We have made peace and moved on from that mistake!"

"You made a lot of work for us," Lily Silverhopper shot back.

"Let's just stop this argument for a moment and plan how we can all work together, especially now that there are plans in the works to incorporate this part of the woods into the Witchland Forest," Sarah said.

"We take care of the valley below and lend our services as needed to the Witchland Forest," Lily

Silverhopper informed her. "Our job is to tend to the plants, animals, fungi, and other beings that call these woods home."

"So, you do exactly what the Leekins do," Sarah commented.

Both the Leekins and the Blackberry Hoppers scoffed violently. "We do it better," Lily Silverhopper replied.

"No, you don't!" the Leekins all cried immediately.

Sarah rolled her eyes. These creatures were starting to get on her nerves. "We can all have our separate duties and territories, but I think we can work together quite well," she interjected.

The Blackberry Hoppers and the Leekins exchanged dirty looks before nodding their heads in agreement.

Just then, Addie let out a joyous bark. Behind the Leekins, Kelvin came trotting up, apparently attracted to the amount of activity in the territory he often roamed. "*I thought I smelled my girl,*" he teased.

Addie ran to him and began to cover his face in licks. "*Look, Sarah, it's my boyfriend!*"

"Very nice." Sarah smiled. She watched the Blackberry Hoppers begin to hop away. *Such fascinating creatures,* she thought. *I'm glad we have some allies, even if they compete a little too much with the Leekins.*

"*Let's race!*" Addie urged. "*You, me, Sarah, and Clover Figcreek.*"

"What about me?" Michael's ghostly voice joined them, and hairs raised along Sarah's back and arms. Sarah no longer minded these ghostly chills, but she still got them whenever Michael's intense electromagnetic energy was near.

"Wow, it's just a little party up here." Sarah laughed.

But Addie had already taken off. She ran alongside Kelvin, whose loping stride seemed to be measured just to give her a fair chance. Clover Figcreek shot off of her pyramid on her wings and disappeared ahead in a brown blur. Sarah and Michael lagged far behind. Sarah ran until she was winded and collapsed on a fallen tree trunk to catch her breath. Michael settled next to her, his energy still somewhat high.

"Aren't you tired? You need more rest than the living," Sarah commented.

Michael merely shrugged. "Since I have no physical body, activities like running don't really require any energy expenditure on my part. I float along and only give the appearance of running, actually. It's quite breezy." He then grinned, the way he always did when he was cracking one of his silly jokes. Sarah had always called him the king of dad jokes.

"I won!" Clover Figcreek declared triumphantly

several minutes later, returning to where Sarah was sitting with Michael. The canines came loping after her, their tongues hanging out of their mouths and their chests heaving with effort.

"Did you just come find me to chat?" Sarah laughed, puzzled. Usually, the Leekins only spoke to her when they wanted something or needed to warn her about something. She still remembered when they broke into her house late at night to rearrange her furniture back to the way Michael had had it. Now she could laugh about it, but at the time, she had really wanted the Leekins to go away.

"Lativia wants to see you. She has something to say." Clover Figcreek assumed her serious affect as the other Leekins all buzzed into the clearing to join her.

Sarah nodded and followed them a short distance to the ghostly clearing. Once she entered the glade, she felt the tingling on her skin grow stronger. Ghosts began to appear around her, disinterested in her presence since her visit did not pertain to them. They carried on, socializing and drinking from cups of glowing blue wine. The clearing's very atmosphere felt charged with electricity, like a lightning bolt had struck nearby.

Suddenly, Lativia Spellwood appeared before them, glowing a pearlescent white and seated on her glowing blue throne. Her long red hair streamed behind her, almost visible through her translucent figure. Though she was extremely pale, it was clear she had once had freckles, just like Sarah. She offered Sarah a slight smile.

Sarah readied herself to receive whatever new enlightenment was coming her way.

CHAPTER FOUR

Sarah realized how much better the mood was this time than during her last meeting with Lativia. The air was light and bright, the sky clear, and the forest free from smoke and evil magical fog that had spread during their epic battle with Madras. Even the natural gloom between the trees was absent, since the leaves were not yet thick enough to block out the sunlight. Things actually felt pleasant, as if nothing might go wrong.

Knock on wood, Sarah thought to herself, rapping her knuckle against the ancient dead oak she was sitting on.

"That is such a useless superstition. It does not work!" Lativia admonished her.

"Force of habit," Sarah said, feeling unsure how to begin this meeting. It was always a surreal experience, speaking to this long-dead witch in this ethereal place. "You have something to tell me? Hopefully nothing bad this time?"

Lativia drifted closer to Sarah. "I wish to praise you, actually. I have been watching your training carefully through my scrying mirror. And I am quite proud of the work you have been doing."

Sarah felt her chest inflate. That was high praise indeed, coming from one of New England's most famous and powerful witches! Though Lativia had been dead for hundreds of years, she still watched over Witchland and worked her magic through living agents such as the Leekins, Jenna the deputy, and Sarah. Her power as a witch was not questionable, even in death. "Hmmm, thank you," she replied, a bit flustered, her cheeks glowing.

"I'm not the only one watching you, either. The fox has been watching you for weeks now. She has something to impart to you," Lativia went on.

"The fox?" Sarah tried to think if she had encountered one, but she would have remembered seeing a fox. She had not seen any of late. Then she thought of the cards she had found littered behind her house, the fox card glaring up at her so obviously. It was a message!

"The fox was one of the last spirit animals who

came to guide me," Lativia said. "I am surprised she is coming to you this early!"

"What—what does it mean that she's coming to me so early?" Sarah leaned forward, her interest piqued.

"She wants something. She has a great deal to offer you. But you have to prove yourself. She is very particular, and will leave if she decides you are not worthy of her time," Lativia advised.

"How can I do that?" Sarah found she often had to prove herself. It often felt like everyone in this place knew things she didn't, and they enjoyed watching her flounder, trying to find her way. She knew that wasn't entirely true, but it was how she often felt, especially after speaking with Lativia. However, that feeling also motivated her, in the same way it did when another lawyer or a client did not think she had it in her to win in the courtroom.

"The fox prides intelligence, wisdom, and cunning. The magic of words over physical magic. The wolf is all power, and you've proved you have power—but can you dance with your words like the fox? You must prove you have the brains for it, or the fox won't reveal herself to you and grant you the gift of her animal spirit guidance."

Sarah bit her lip. "Interesting. I can see that being important as a lawyer, too—maybe she is watching how

I work? How is she even watching me, if I haven't seen her?"

"You won't see her, at least not in the way you think. Deliberately seeking her out will only drive her farther away; she will come to you only when she wishes. She is a trickster, though, always up to harmless mischief because she likes to have fun and to test others. Her affinity for shock value is all part of her mystique." Lativia smiled fondly, clearly remembering her own fox guide with love.

"What about the cards?" Sarah reached into her pocket and pulled them out. She held up the fox card.

"I didn't use cards," Lativia admitted. Sarah had never heard her say that she did not work in a particular type of magic. "That is a very new set of animal oracle cards. You must find someone who can read them and learn what they mean."

"You didn't plant them? And the fox didn't?" Sarah demanded.

"Not I." Lativia shook her head. "And the fox would not be that obvious."

"*I smelled a human,*" Addie spoke up.

"I can point you to someone," Michael spoke up. "She does divination, card readings. She might know more about this. Maybe she's even the one who planted these?"

Sarah nodded. "I want to see her. I didn't know

there was someone who did divination here in town—other than you, Lativia. That's a magical skill I haven't learned yet."

Lativia waved her hand. "Rely on your own intuition, not silly cards! I didn't use cards in my day."

"Cards help you get to know yourself more than getting to know the future," Michael responded. "They give you perspective and ideas about a situation, but they don't make decisions for you. They aren't so much for divination themselves, though Frida Pecto is quite good at that. She has this party trick, reading tea leaves. It creeps people out!"

"Frida Pecto." Sarah smiled. "Sounds like a new mentor to me. Will you direct me to her house, please?"

"Of course! Follow me," Michael responded.

Sarah turned to Lativia. "Is there anything else I need to know?"

"Just be your best self and keep a clear head," Lativia advised. "Watch out for the fox. Sooner or later, she may reveal herself to you, and what she will have to say is very valuable. But if you're not watching out for her, she might slip by, unnoticed, and her wisdom is a terrible thing to waste. Like all your animal guides, the fox has answers to your questions."

"Thank you, Lativia," Sarah said respectfully.

Lativia nodded graciously and began to fade into

the surroundings, returning to her place of spiritual rest.

Michael began to lead everyone down the mountain. He intended to show Sarah where Frida the diviner lived, but they were interrupted by a dark blue Leekin hurrying up the path to meet them.

"Flora McLeafy!" Clover Figcreek cried. "What's the matter?"

Sarah wondered at how Leekins managed to be so fast, yet still not out of breath and tired. They were such an odd species. They were worth some serious biological examination, but who would believe her enough to examine them? And would any of the Leekins consent to being examined? They were a rather querulous bunch, extremely persnickety about everything. Sarah had long since learned to just accept their idiosyncrasies and avoid provoking them into their wailing, quivering drama.

"It's the Hunter!" Flora gasped out.

All of the Leekins began the shivering and wailing that Sarah despised. Even Addie backed away from them, finding their high-pitched cries painful to her sensitive ears. Kelvin looked annoyed and said, "*What is the point of all that driveling, really? Just do something about it instead of whining about it!*"

But this time, Sarah didn't have time to feel annoyed, because her soul was shaking with terror.

"Wait . . . you mean Dismas? Dismas Lorian?" she demanded, wondering how on earth he had gotten out of prison.

"No! Oscar!" Flora McLeafy replied.

"I thought he went away to live in Maine," moaned Clover Figcreek.

"I saw him! Opening up the hunting lodge! He's back!" Flora continued. "And he was carrying a big rifle and a crossbow on his back."

"Oh, no," Clover Figcreek moaned. "He's back to kill our fauna. This is bad, very, very bad!" She began to wring her hands fervently, flying back and forth in a Leekin version of pacing.

Sarah felt her stomach tighten with adrenaline. "Oscar Reedy?" She blinked in confusion. "I didn't know you also called him the Hunter."

"There are many Hunters, bad men who hurt our woods," Clover Figcreek explained in a voice squeaky with panic. "That Oscar man brings them in here! That makes him the ultimate Hunter!"

"You know Oscar Reedy?" Michael asked Sarah.

"No, I just know he owns the Witchland Hunting Lodge and Guide Service. I know the holders of all of the property deeds in the area," Sarah answered. "I also know that he was good friends with Dismas Lorian, though he has never crossed my radar as a trou-blemaker."

"He is a troublemaker because he kills our animals! Then stuffs them and mounts them on his walls! He leads other bad men and hunters into the part of the forest where we were earlier, where hunting is legal," Flora McLeafy informed Sarah as she quaked in fear.

"He left to open another lodge in Maine not long before you moved here," Michael added. "It is odd that he's back. Maybe he heard rumors that the town plans to acquire that patch of forest? It won't bode satisfactorily for his business, though."

"We have to go check this out," Sarah urged Michael, Addie, and Kelvin.

"*Nope, I'm out,*" Kelvin said. Fear showed through his normally casual, charming personality. "*They have my aunt's head mounted on the wall,*" he added when everyone appraised him quizzically. "*I'm not going anywhere near that house of horrors.*"

Sarah felt bad. "I'm sorry," she told him. Addie ran up and licked him comfortingly.

He agreed to hide in the woods near the lodge with the Leekins and stay within earshot in case they needed him. Sarah and Addie, accompanied by an invisible ghostly Michael, hiked up to the lodge. Sarah felt nervous, wondering how this man would act. *Is this going to be another Dismas scenario?* she wondered with a shudder. Flashbacks to her harrowing encounter with Dismas, where he had almost killed her and then later had almost killed Addie, filled her mind.

"Don't worry, I will drive him away if he tries to hurt you!" Addie assured her.

The hunting lodge was a gorgeous log cabin set in the hills near where Sarah had run into Flora McLeafy. From the outside, it looked like any other cabin. But inside, it was an opulent lodge with a rustic theme. As she entered, she breathed in the scent of wood lacquer and smoke from a fireplace. She first noticed a social area with overstuffed couches centered around a table with a checkerboard, before a large stone fireplace in which flames licked over crackling logs. A huge flat-screen TV played a poker tournament. The walls were adorned with the mounted heads of wildlife claimed within the forest, their glass eyes staring down with disquieting stillness. A polished wooden spiral staircase led up into an open upstairs area with five doors, obviously the guest rooms.

"Sarah Spellwood!" Sarah started at a voice and turned to see a man approaching her with his arms outspread. He was dressed head to toe in camouflage, and his beard was neatly combed. He looked to be in his mid-sixties, with a large, shiny bald spot in the center of his head. "How nice to finally meet you!"

Sarah stepped back in concern before realizing that the man truly was brimming with friendly warmth.

She then recognized that she had seen him at the mayoral debate. He had been one of the particularly vocal people in opposition of Roger Miller and Hua. "Oscar Reedy, hello. Pleasure to make your acquaintance." She offered him her hand, which he shook warmly.

"Boy, that mayoral debate sure was something, wasn't it?" Oscar laughed. His own dog, a spotted coonhound ran up to Addie to exchange sniffs with her. "Meet my dog Geronimo."

"Addie, be polite," Sarah said cautiously as Addie promptly began to sniff Geronimo's behind.

"*What?*" Addie exclaimed. "*I am just seeing what he ate earlier.*"

Oscar laughed, watching the two dogs sniff one another. "Tell me, what do you think?"

"About what? Oh, about the debate?" Sarah sighed. "The town sure seems divided over it."

"I would love to see us acquire more land, but then I'm sure they would make it a no-hunting area. I have to say, I think Malorie is onto something," Oscar went on. "Though I must admit, she and I have had our differences. She has never liked me. I think maybe because she sees me as competition, you know? But we really cater to entirely different types of guests."

Sarah nodded, unwilling to get into a political debate with the large, brawny man who clearly saw the world very differently than she did. While she did not have a problem with hunting for food or Oscar Reedy, she knew that her veganism and animal-rights-activist mentality was a world away from his.

"Tell me, what can I do for you today, Miss Spellwood?" Oscar finally asked, realizing that she wasn't taking his bait for a discussion about Witchland's next mayor.

"I just heard you were back in town, and I wanted to meet you," Sarah said. She watched him for a reaction and was relieved to see that he did not seem to consider her an enemy right off the bat.

"I have certainly wanted to meet you, as well. You know, I admire what you did, putting away Dismas. He was actually a good friend of mine. He stayed here countless times, so much that I left him a key to this place when I went to Maine because I trusted him so much." He shook his head grimly. "I was horrified to learn what he did." Oscar looked genuinely sympathetic as he placed a meaty hand on Sarah's shoulder. "I am sure sorry about your friend, Michael Howler. I didn't know him too well, but he was a good man."

Sarah smiled, relaxing under the weight of Oscar's hand. "Thank you. I am glad you don't have any hard feelings against me about Dismas."

"Oh, of course not! I lost one of my best customers"—he let out a short laugh before removing his hand and sobering—"but he deserves to be in prison. I don't support criminals, nor do I support unethical hunters like that. Guys like that give us all a bad name. Then people want to ban hunting for good and take away our firearms because they think we're all violent sociopaths!"

"You know, I wanted to ask you about that," Sarah said, testing the water.

Oscar narrowed his eyes slightly, clearly readying himself to defend his hunting if need be. "About what, Miss Spellwood?"

"I just wanted to ensure that you are obeying all hunting laws and not going after endangered animals. It is my duty as a Witchlander to protect the flora and fauna of these woods," Sarah said.

Oscar looked taken aback. "Of course I obey all hunting laws. I only hunt animals that are not on the endangered species list, and I only hunt during the appropriate seasons. I have a business to worry about; I can't jeopardize my guide license."

Sarah glanced up at his walls and caught sight of a mounted lynx. "What about that lynx?" She pointed. "Lynx are protected in these woods."

Oscar looked irritated. "Now, I shot that lynx in 1987, long before the lynx were endangered in these woods. I pride myself on being an ethical hunter, Miss

Spellwood. Frankly, I'm becoming quite offended by this line of questioning."

"It's only wild turkey season right now," Michael whispered in her ear. "Starting tomorrow, May 1st."

"What do you have right now, a turkey tag?" she asked.

"Of course!" He shrugged. "Why do you ask?"

"I am just wondering because I have a special interest in protecting the foxes, and I want to make sure they're not being hunted." Oscar had such a kind face that she couldn't believe he was capable of wrongdoing and poaching, but she also had to remember Flora McLeafy's and Clover Figcreek's reactions to his presence. Clearly, something was amiss about him being here.

He gasped incredulously. "Foxes? They're not illegal to hunt. They're not even endangered!"

Sarah shook her head. "I understand that fact, but their numbers are dwindling because of distemper introduced by feral dogs. The laws haven't caught up yet, so I have to do my part in protecting them."

Oscar laughed shortly. "Let me tell you something, you're not the one making the laws just because you like foxes."

This comment rankled Sarah, but she knew he was completely right. As she rapidly thought of her counterargument and how to protect her future spirit animal, Michael whispered in her ear, "Tell him you're planning to make foxes a protected species."

"I'm actually filing paperwork to make the red fox protected. In the meantime, I will be watching to see if you or any of your hunters break any hunting laws, just to protect the foxes until the paperwork goes through," she informed Oscar.

Oscar snorted angrily, his nostrils flaring and his cheeks flushing. "My, my, I sure wish city folk like you didn't get it into your heads to come up here and then try to change this town. Things were just fine before you arrived, and they will be fine when you finally get bored and leave. How about you go along now and leave me be?"

"I won't ever get bored trying to defend the creatures of this forest. This is my home, and I am going to protect these woods," Sarah replied.

Oscar now looked incensed. "I think it might be best if you go now. I don't think we have anything else to talk about. You act like I'm doing something wrong, when I'm not."

"I'm not trying to accuse you of anything," Sarah attempted to say.

But Oscar had already had enough. He pointed at the door. "Don't ever try to mess with my livelihood," he growled.

Sarah made a point of walking out slowly with

Addie by her side so that Oscar did not think he had intimidated her. Oscar slammed the door behind her, making her jump.

"That was great!" Michael crowed once they were a short way from the lodge. "Like old times!"

Sarah couldn't help but flush in embarrassment. "It seems I've made an enemy now. I should have been more delicate, but that's how I get sometimes."

Just then, a red flash caught Sarah's eye. The fox! Her heart began hammering as she shouted, "Wait! Fox, wait!" She began to chase it.

The fox paused and looked over its shoulder at her, its eyes twinkling. Then it twitched its tail and shot off into the underbrush. Sarah attempted to circumvent the patch of brush it had disappeared into, but her arms and legs wound up tangled in some branches.

Michael and Addie helped her untangle herself. She looked around frantically and called for the fox, but it was gone.

"That's a great sign! The fox showed itself to you!" Michael congratulated her.

But Sarah shook her head. "She didn't like what I said to Oscar. That's why she ran and hid from me. I really need to hear what she has to say to me. This is incredibly discouraging."

"It's still progress," Michael said helpfully.

"No, it's a bad sign. I think it's because you had to

guide me." Sarah groaned in frustration. "I should have done all of that on my own and listened to my instincts about Oscar, instead of listening to you. I won't grow as a lawyer or a witch if everyone keeps helping me. I need to do this on my own."

"On your own? Remember how much you needed our help with Madras Spellwood?" Addie admonished her.

"I don't mean entirely on my own," Sarah corrected herself. "But I need more space to grow. I need you to stop mentoring me, Michael." She turned to face his ghost, feeling terrible about what she had to say. "I need to think for myself more and get on my own two feet."

"You don't want my mentorship anymore?" Michael sounded heartbroken.

"I do, and I feel terrible for what I just said to you. I just need some time to grow and figure things out on my own," Sarah replied. "It's not that I don't want your help . . . but I need you to not step in when I am in a situation like that." As she tried to explain, however, she realized that she had already hurt him and there was no going back.

"Oh." Michael looked dejected. "I'm going to go rest, then."

"Michael! I am sorry. Please don't go. Your help is

needed," Sarah begged, already feeling guilty as Michael's outline faded into oblivion.

"That was kind of mean," Addie said reproachfully, looking at Sarah with large, sad eyes.

"I know. I have to make things right with Michael," Sarah replied feebly. But she wondered how to do that now. "I made Michael feel useless, and that's the last thing I wanted to do to him."

"He will forgive you. You just have to ask for his help again and make him feel useful,"

Addie suggested helpfully.

Sarah smiled. "That's a good idea. I'll find something he can help with."

CHAPTER FIVE

MICHAEL DID NOT COME TO SPEAK TO SARAH FOR A few days, so she had to ask Daisy where Frida lived.

Daisy was busy as usual, whipping up a bald-spot-be-gone potion for a customer before closing time. "Frida Pecto?" she asked, appearing surprised. "That woman is a charlatan. What do you want to see her for?"

"Why do you say she's a charlatan?" Sarah asked, stunned by Daisy's uncharacteristic brusqueness. "Michael and Lativia actually want me to speak with her."

Daisy pursed her lips. "Just one of those women who may have had a gift, but now she's so commercialized, it's hard to tell. She dresses up like a Gypsy, even though she is clearly Norwegian! Crystal balls and all of that." She waved her hand with disgust. "It may work on the men, but not on me!"

Sarah got the distinct feeling that there was more to the story. "Are you willing to send me her way?"

"I suppose." Daisy begrudgingly scribbled Frida's address on the back of one of her business cards. "Don't tell her I sent you her way. I don't want her thinking I am referring people to her now and that we're all chummy."

"Thanks." Sarah tucked the card into her pocket. "You sure don't seem to care for her. Is there maybe another reason why?"

Daisy merely pursed her lips and shook her head, her long dreads swinging. "Ancient history."

"All right, but please tell me how things are, otherwise?" Sarah prodded.

Daisy chuckled and shook her head. "Oddest thing, actually. I misplaced my lucky potion vial."

"Lucky potion vial?" Sarah leaned forward, her curiosity piqued. Something Harriet had said about a lucky bauble the other day flitted across her mind.

"My mother enchanted it with good luck years ago and gave it to me when I came of age and was first initiated into magic. She told me to keep it on me always, so I keep it clipped to my herb pouch that I carry everywhere I go. I never take it off. Only now it's gone." She sighed sadly. "I keep hoping it'll turn up, but no such luck. I hope it didn't fall off somewhere and shatter."

"When did you last see it?" Sarah inquired.

"I thought I saw it last night, before my shower. But this morning, it was gone. I didn't go anywhere last night, which is why this is all incredibly strange." Daisy shook her head. "I'm way too young and healthy to be going senile!" she attempted to joke. But Sarah could tell this event was weighing on her.

"Addie, can you maybe sniff it out?" Sarah asked.

Addie ran around the shop sniffing for it with no luck. The two offered to keep a lookout for it. "*I won't chew on it too much if we find it,*" Addie vowed.

"Tons of thanks. Don't exhaust yourselves looking for it. I'm sure you have better things to do," Daisy said, embarrassment creeping into her voice. Sarah knew how much Daisy hated asking for help, as much as Sarah loved helping others.

Sarah hugged Daisy goodbye and jaunted toward Frida's fortune parlor, which Daisy said was tacky and catered to the tourists. Just as she passed the town hall, she heard shouting and smelled a whiff of smoke, which awoke bad memories for her from the previous fall's forest fire.

"Hey!" she shouted, bolting into the town hall.

Eli was already standing in the town clerk's office with the new town clerk, Alex, who had replaced Peter

Atticos after his murder the previous fall. He was holding a Class C fire extinguisher, and the foam cloud from its recent blast was settling over the office, burying the small fire that had broken out on Alex's desk. The smell of smoke turned into a strong chemical odor that offended Addie, making her run back outside.

"Are you guys all right?" Sarah demanded.

Eli put a protective arm around her and guided her toward the open window. "It seems to be an electrical short. The fire is out for now, but we need to get the electrical company down here ASAP."

"I started my computer and the cord just started flashing and then burning!" Alex looked flustered and sheepish as she attempted to smooth her brown pixie cut.

"I'm just glad you didn't get hurt! And it looks like nothing much was harmed." Sarah glanced around the little office. She was glad to see it free from crime scene tape and black fingerprint dust. Bad memories from poor Mr. Atticos's murder made her stomach knot up.

Alex let out a dark laugh that was shaky with her adrenaline. "I swear! I've just been having the worst luck lately, ever since my lucky horseshoe turned up missing."

Sarah wheeled to face her. "Your lucky horseshoe?"

These similarities were possibly just coincidence,

but Sarah knew coincidences tended to be much more in Witchland. How had three women lost their lucky charms in the span of a few days?

Alex shuffled her feet and gave a feeble laugh, trying to hide her blush. "It may sound silly, but . . . my grandparents used to live here. They believed in all that Spellwood stuff."

Sarah glanced down. Clearly, Alex, who was a newcomer to the town, did not know Sarah's last name or her lineage yet.

"Anyway, they said that horseshoe was lucky and gave it to me when I left for college. I always have it near me. And I had it hanging there." Alex led them back into the smoldering office and pointed to a tiny nail protruding from the wooden wall across from her desk. "Now it's gone. Poof."

Eli ran his thumb over the nail. "Odd. It didn't just fall down?" He stooped to glance under her desk in case it had fallen and slid under there and stood back up, perplexed. "I can tell you it's not under there."

"No. I've looked everywhere. Since that went missing, my whole day has been a mess! Nothing has gone right! And to make matters worse, my boyfriend canceled his weekend plans to drive up here and spend time with me. Said he had a work thing he couldn't get out of." Alex looked a bit distraught. "I don't believe in luck, but I have to wonder . . ." She

shook her head, trying to clear her mind of the superstition.

"You would be surprised what is real here and what is not," Sarah commented vaguely. Could Alex be a possible new initiate into the secrets of Witch-land? Many lived here without ever knowing the secrets—but others came here because they were meant to find out the magical powers hidden within their spirits.

Eli shot Sarah a sympathetic look, then turned to Alex. "We understand that you're new to the town and don't know many people. If you ever want to join us for coffee and pastries at Javacadabra, just let us know."

Alex looked pleased and rubbed her hands together. "I love their blackberry cheese muffins! Best I've ever had! Can we take a break now?"

The trio headed to the café after ensuring the fire was out, Addie trotting behind them complaining about the stench from the fire. Eli made Alex promise not to turn anything electric on the next day until the electric company and fire marshal had conducted a safety inspection. Neither of them would be willing to drive to Witchland this late, not even after a small fire. "Time moves so slowly here!" Alex wondered aloud, shaking her head and laughing. "I am from a much bigger city."

"Boston?" Sarah asked.

"You could tell by my accent." Alex grinned.

"One thing is for sure, Witchland takes some getting used to after you come from a big city," Sarah agreed. "But you'll come to love it."

"I kind of do already. I love the quiet and the hiking," Alex said, her face lighting up. "I like having a good job, too. It was hard to find clerical work in Boston with no experience. You'd think finding a job in the big city would be easy, but not when you're a rather noncompetitive person like me. It's just painfully hard to talk myself up in interviews the way they expect, you know?"

Sarah smiled, trying not to think of the crushing competition she had endured leaving law school and job hunting among the top firms. That had not been a great time in her life, and she had rapidly changed from a starry-eyed graduate to a jaded adult. The only things that had placated her then were Michael and Jeff. Jeff, at one time, had been a loving, supportive husband—until resentment of Sarah's success took the place of his affection. Somehow, she had made it through that tough year, and had landed a great job at a top firm based on her experience working in legal aid in law school.

The trio settled into seats at Javacadabra, placed their orders, and began to talk about Witchland.

"This place is weird. Like . . . is everyone really that obsessed with witches?" Alex asked.

Sarah and Eli exchanged brief smirks. "Um, it's a bit of the town's history, yes," Eli finally answered diplomatically.

"Wow, super weird! Why celebrate a history like that?" Alex shuddered. "My grandparents were sure into some spooky stuff. Mostly plants, but sometimes they talked about spells."

Sarah smiled. "My grandmother and my aunt were like that, too, but my parents forbade it." She fondly thought back to her aunt Beth Spellwood's gigantic house, with its rooms full of strange instruments and ceremonial robes and books. Her grandparents had also lived there, leaving behind many magical items and traditions when they passed before Sarah was born. Sarah had heard many stories of their magical powers from Aunt Beth. What a treasure trove that house surely contained! But her parents had sold it all in an estate sale after Aunt Beth had passed. Mostly Spellwood legend-obsessed collectors bought the items, or so Sarah had thought at the time; now she wondered how many of those buyers may have been magically inclined themselves. Sarah had grown up very sheltered from her magical background, connecting to it only when she visited Aunt Beth and had conversations with her pet goat. When Aunt Beth passed, Sarah removed herself from magic completely in order to fit in at school. She was a complete skeptic until Michael bequeathed to her his firm and house. Perhaps Alex now faced the same journey?

"And now? What do you believe?" Alex asked Sarah, studying her.

Sarah shrugged and exchanged laughs with Eli. "Witchland changes you."

An awkward silence fell over the table. Finally, Alex cleared her throat and said, "Thank you. I feel much better now." She held up the paper from her blackberry cheese muffin. "These always seem to do the trick."

"Karen's baking is magic in itself," Eli agreed with her, smiling pleasantly. "We'll get that short taken care of, don't you worry."

Alex beamed. "Everyone here is very nice. Thank you!" Then she scooted out of the booth and slung her purse strap over her shoulder. "I had better go grab my files from the office and finish my work on my laptop at home. My boyfriend will hopefully want to do a Zoom call after his meeting," she added, looking less than hopeful.

After she had bobbed off, skipping slightly in her flats, Sarah sighed. "She almost reminds me of myself when I first came here."

"It's eerie," Eli agreed. "But you're prettier," he

added, leaning over to plant a kiss on her cheek.

"I wasn't jealous." Sarah giggled. "But I don't mind hearing how much you like me. I could listen to you tell me that all day."

"Well then." He cupped her cheek in his palm and brought her face up so he could stare into her eyes. "You are not only the most beautiful woman in the world, but also the only one who truly scares me. That is no easy feat."

The two laughed and rubbed noses before kissing. Addie groaned under the table, *"Get a room!"* Addie tended to have less tolerance for their romance when Kelvin wasn't around to give her the same kind of attention.

"Weird thing, Daisy and Harriet have been missing their good luck charms, too," Sarah said when they broke apart.

"That's weird. Are you saying these things are somehow linked?" Eli frowned in thought.

"Possibly? I mean, it seems like an odd coincidence." Sarah shrugged. "Could be nothing, but it's worth watching out for."

"But who would steal little trinkets? And why? You of all people know charms aren't real magic," Eli mused.

Sarah smiled. "You know from the deed that Lativia enchanted to protect this town that any object can be made magical. I'm positive Daisy's vial is magical, anyway, and probably Alex's, judging by her grandparents. Harriet, I don't even know. I have heard she's a powerful witch, but I haven't seen it firsthand. Geez, I wonder who Alex's grandparents are?"

"The Greenes. Their house sat empty forever until Alex moved in. I have heard stories; they were pretty wild with the magic stuff." Eli laughed.

"Interesting. I think Alex might have powers. And I think this person—whoever it is—is targeting witches, taking their luck away." Sarah bit her lip as she thought her theory over.

"I'll keep an ear open for other incidents," Eli agreed.

Susie brought the bill. Eli produced his card, but she said, "Sorry, our credit card machine has been down all morning."

"No problem." Sarah opened her purse and began to scrounge for change. She had a few bills and coins. Eli added what he had in his wallet.

"A penny short." Eli frowned. "I'm really sorry."

"Don't worry about it." Susie laughed, waving her hand casually. "It's just a penny."

Zeva yawned on the counter and said, *"Next time, bring me treats. I like the salmon kind."*

"What are the chances?" Sarah whispered to Eli as

they exited the little café. "I mean, that never happens to us!"

"It was just a penny. You really think it has that much to do with luck?" Eli, always the doubter, looked hesitant.

"It just seems like a weird pattern today, bad luck for everyone all around. And I meant to go see this woman, but I guess it's too late now," Sarah said as she noticed the falling twilight.

"Who?" Eli asked.

"Frida Pecto. The fortune-teller."

"Oh. I really don't know her that well." Eli put his hand on Sarah's back as he walked her to her cottage. "She did used to be engaged to Earl Reid, who was actually Daisy's former fiancé, too," he added.

"Now that makes a lot of sense; Daisy acted so sullen when I mentioned her." Sarah laughed. "Honestly, I never imagined Daisy to be the jealous type."

"They have had a bit of a rivalry over the years. I don't know much about it. Neither of those ladies cause any trouble, so they don't cross my path very often," Eli said.

Sarah smiled and pecked his cheek. "I must be a troublemaker, to always cross your path."

"You sure are," he teased, snuggling her close. "Tell me, why do you want to see Frida?"

Sarah pulled the animal cards out of her pocket. Eli

went through them, shaking his head. "And someone just left these in your bushes? Addie can't tell who?"

"Nope, she just says it's an off-smelling human being." Sarah took the cards back. "The person must know something about my animal spirit guides, you know, which you and I were talking about the other day. But I don't know what. Since Frida reads cards, maybe she can help. Lativia thinks she can, anyway."

"One thing is for sure, if Lativia thinks so, then you should go talk to her," Eli agreed.

"I hope that she's the one who planted them. Otherwise, I have a long mystery ahead of me." Sarah sighed.

"Stop it, you love mysteries," Eli chided her. "You are always reading them and thrusting yourself into every mystery in town."

Sarah grinned. "You got me there."

They paused on Sarah's doorstep. "This is all really weird. Will you go with me to talk to people about their good luck charms? I just have a feeling this is not simply three isolated incidents here," Sarah begged him.

"Maybe, if I get a kiss," he teased.

Precisely at that moment, Michael made his presence felt. "*It's not chance,*" he warned in his faraway, ghostly voice.

"*What is it then?*" Sarah asked him telepathically.

"*You didn't want my help,*" he replied petulantly. It was clear he was still sore about their tiff in the forest.

Sarah sighed. "*Michael, really, I'm so sorry about that,*" she told him. "*You know that I love you more than anything, and I will always need your help.*"

He was quiet for a moment. Sarah waited for his reply, while Eli looked at her as if she were crazy. "Are you having some sort of witchy moment?" he asked slowly.

"Yes." She nodded with a laugh.

Michael finally said, "*I don't want to interrupt your date, but it has to do with the fox. The fox is stealing the charms.*"

Sarah thanked Michael profusely before turning to Eli. "Come inside," she urged Eli, pulling him into the house while playing with the top button of his shirt.

"Tell me something. Is the witchy moment over?" Eli joked.

CHAPTER SIX

Feeling refreshed and loved the next morning, Sarah decided to jog over to Frida's and finish what she had been unable to the night before. She was filled with burning curiosity for what this fortune-teller might have to say. She and Addie headed off to her house.

Frida's small home was painted the color of cinnamon, and the scent of incense poured through the cracks in the windows, which were framed in orange. When Sarah entered the front room, she was surprised by the sheer overdecoration of it—fluffy ottomans, peacock feathers fanned across the ceiling, bead curtains sparkling in every doorway, strange art and framed poetry covering every inch of wall space, gleaming crystals resting on every surface, statues standing boldly in every corner. An enormous dragon tapestry hung above a table draped in red brocade, where incense was burning in a gilt holder shaped like a koi fish. The room was a strange fusion of Asian Buddhist and Gypsy fortune-teller, making Sarah feel slightly disoriented. The incense was heady and over-powering.

The bead curtain leading into the back of the house rustled, and Frida bustled out, looking every bit as overdone as her room. Sarah couldn't help but notice the excessive rouge Frida wore. And smudged kohl. She did look like a woman trying to play a part in a circus rather than a real witch. Maybe Daisy was right and Frida was a charlatan? Sarah wondered why Lativia had sent her here if that was the case.

"Hi!" Frida welcomed Sarah, ushering her into a stuffed chair. "I've been waiting for you!"

"Have you?" Sarah always felt so disconcerted when people said that, like Daisy the first day Sarah had visited her at the apothecary begging for magic lessons. If these witches wanted to meet her that badly, why didn't they come see her? They knew exactly where she lived.

"I sense you found my cards. Or rather, she did." Frida winked at Addie, who sat obediently at Sarah's side. As soon as she turned her attention to Addie, though, Addie went to her, wagging her tail and panting for scratches.

"*She's nice!*" Addie told Sarah.

"Ahhh . . . so it was you who planted these cards?" Sarah asked. "Why?" She removed them from her pocket and laid them on the brocade-covered table.

"I didn't plant these. They were stolen from me," Frida replied calmly.

Sarah perked up. "Stolen? Really? Would they happen to be good luck cards for you?"

Frida laughed and shook her head. "No, no, not good luck. They're animal spirit cards. I read them for clients who want to learn their animal spirit team that will help guide them in life. But I sensed they were stolen for a higher purpose, and I see that is true now, since they led you to me."

"So you have no idea who stole them?" Sarah felt that now she definitely had a mystery on her hands to solve. All of these thefts probably weren't just random crimes; they served some sort of agenda. Why else would the thief target good luck charms and animal spirit cards?

Frida smiled and shrugged. "I had four people come in for readings that day; they disappeared after my last client."

"Who was that client?" Sarah sat on the edge of her seat in anticipation.

"Susan Lake, actually." Frida laughed. "If you would believe that."

"No, I don't believe that." Sarah frowned. "Why would Susan Lake steal these?"

"I don't believe she would, but that is beyond my divination powers. Someone took these to bring you to me. They knew we could work together," Frida said proudly.

"I do look forward to that," Sarah admitted. "I haven't learned divination at all. Can you tell me, what do these cards mean?" Sarah asked.

Frida tapped the first card with her long nail, which was embellished with a gold jewel at the tip. "The wolf. You know what this one means deep in your heart."

"Are you—are you a part of the Wolf Coven?" Sarah ventured.

Frida laughed airily. "Not at all, honey. I don't practice magic, only clairvoyance. But I have great respect for you gals of the magical Wolf Coven!"

"Isn't clairvoyance magic?" Sarah was confused.

"Not really. It's just sensitivity to knowledge we all have, but most of us choose to shun that knowledge because it's difficult to process. I, on the other hand, welcome it." Frida cleared her throat and folded her hands on the table. "To be honest with you, it sells pretty well. I love reading people's card spreads. And I designed these cards to tap into the animal spirits that so many people aren't aware they are being guided by.

When you gain an animal as your spirit guide, you essentially share all of the characteristics of that animal, and often a member of the particular species will personally appear and offer you protection or guidance."

"You only do these readings for the money?" Sarah asked, her opinion of the woman growing slightly more negative.

Frida looked slightly defensive. "We all have to make a living somehow, darling. Your dear friend Daisy uses her magic for money, too."

Sarah relented. Frida had a valid point.

"I had a calling the other day that you have reached a point in your magical journey where you need some guidance, some guidance that comes from within." Now Frida tapped on the lynx card. "Your animal spirit guides. You need them now more than ever, and it's time you learned about them and opened your heart to them."

"It's a weird coincidence, because my boyfriend brought that up. Animal spirit guides. He wanted me to get a book out of the library," Sarah mused. "And Lativia says that I should be acquiring the fox soon, if I do the right thing."

Frida smiled mysteriously. "You don't need to check that book out, because I have it right here for you." She produced a thick book from under the folds of the table's brocade cloth.

Sarah groaned, discouraged by the sight of another massive volume encased in library film. "I am reading so much dense material on environmental law, I can't possibly read all that before it's due. And I might forget to check it back in." Then she paused and glanced at Frida, chills running up and down her spine. "You knew Eli wanted me to check this out?"

"There are no coincidences, honey. Your gut has been telling you lately about something, hasn't it?" Frida smiled knowingly as she laid the book on the table. "You can wait on the book. It contains nothing you don't already know deep in your heart somewhere. But I want to do an animal oracle reading on you, if you will allow me."

"Does—does Lativia know you do this?" Sarah glanced at the unfamiliar cards doubtfully.

"She doesn't care for cards; she thinks they're silly," Frida answered. "But as I said, I don't practice Spell-wood magic."

"Sure, I would like a reading, then." Sarah laid her hands on the table.

"Wonderful! These are the cards I drew on you before you arrived." She spread the cards out in a fan. "The wolf, the lynx, the crow, and the fox. These are your animal spirit guides; this is your team. There are two more, as every person has six animal spirit guides, but I can't detect what they are for you yet; they're waiting to reveal themselves." She smiled down at Addie, who was leaning against her leg, lapping up her attention. "You have already become acquainted with three of these members of your team, right?"

"Yes, and now I'm trying to speak with the fox, but she keeps evading me," Sarah responded. She wondered briefly about when and where she might encounter the last two animals and what they were.

"What do these animals mean to you exactly?" Frida asked Sarah, boring into her with her astute eyes.

Sarah felt spiritually naked under Frida's gaze. This woman really was perceptive. "I think the wolf is my heart . . . my courage." She thought back to her first transformation into a wolf on Mount Katribus, how terrifying yet exhilarating it had been. "The lynx is my spirit, powerful but shy. The crow represents my good intentions, and how I can be misunderstood at times. And the fox is my shrewdness. I need to get in closer with the fox to untangle whatever is going on in this town right now."

"The fox is only making mischief to draw your attention to something within you," Frida answered. "She wants you to learn a valuable lesson, one you can only learn by yourself."

Sarah nodded, internalizing the message. "Could

she be the one committing all of these thefts?" she wondered.

Frida smiled knowingly. "If that is what you think, then it is probably worth some investigation, don't you agree?"

"I will certainly investigate it." Sarah nodded. "But Lativia told me that the fox will try to evade me if I look for her too hard. I don't know how to follow her and see if she's committed these thefts."

"That is something you must ponder." Frida retrieved another deck of cards, which she explained were the persona deck. "These represent what aspects of your personality the animals relate to. You want to look at what I draw and make your own inferences. I will only draw four, since I only drew four animals on you thus far. But just so you know, there are actually twenty-five cards in a full reading." She then drew cards depicting a hero, leader, hunter, and explorer. "What do these mean to you?" she asked Sarah, contemplating them with her sharp blue eyes.

Sarah squirmed in her seat. "I hate to be immodest, but I guess I worked with some other witches and became the town's hero. My goal is to be the hero all of the time, too. I want to save these woods from development, from greed." She touched the shiny surface of the card, marveling at its accuracy. "I'm not much of a leader yet, but I try to be, especially in my field. Paranormal law, environmental law. And I am exploring magic for the first time in my life. I love exploring the woods, too. The hunter . . . I think that is because I'm so passionate for animal life."

"That is very insightful. I'm glad you are becoming in tune with yourself, as not many people are. That's why they pay me money to tell them their inner selves, their futures." Frida grinned bittersweetly. "Sometimes, I wish I could guide people to be more at one with themselves, but such is the life of a fortune-teller."

"You don't feel that you are doing something wrong by telling people things they should know?" Sarah asked. "After all, what if you're wrong?"

Frida smiled. "I always clarify that the future is never concrete, that what I read is only one outcome that is likely to happen if someone keeps treading the path they are on. Any decision can change the whole course of one's life, for better or for worse. I tend to base my readings more upon what someone feels or what is going on in someone's present. This way they can make their own decisions. If I get a strong warning, such as that the person may die tomorrow, I use my discretion in whether or not I tell them that." She looked down sharply. "Usually, I don't tell people bad news, unless I get a calling that they need to hear the message—this way they can reshape their destinies. I don't like to cause people stress when it comes to events they can't help."

Frida then pulled out a second deck. "Anyway, back to our reading. These are your color cards. They also tell a lot about where you are right now, spiritually, mentally, emotionally. They can point you toward problems in your life that you need to fix, or things that bring you joy. Again, it is your interpretation, not mine." Then she read the colors pink, orange, green, and yellow.

"I'm really not sure what these mean for me." Sarah finally shrugged, stumped.

"Then tell me, what associations do you have with these colors?" Frida asked. She drew her ornate nails along the borders of the cards. "They must speak to you in some way."

"Hmmm . . . pink, to me, is all about love," Sarah began hesitantly. The other colors boggled her mind.

"What kind of love? Maternal, romantic, platonic?" Frida urged.

"All of those, I guess." Sarah glanced down at Addie. "I'm surrounded by people and creatures I love right now. And I love this town."

Frida smiled. "Very good. The others?"

"Orange . . ." All Sarah could think of was orange popsicles, summer sun, fun in the pool when she was a kid. "Fun, I guess? Though I don't see how that applies here."

"Of course it applies. Maybe you need more fun in your life. Or maybe you are having fun?"

Sarah nodded. "I am, more than I ever have in my life. Most definitely, the green would be for Witchland, the woods, and the life here. When I think of Witchland, I think of its greenness."

Frida tapped the last card, yellow. "And what about this one?"

"Hmmm . . . all I can think of is a yield sign," Sarah answered slowly.

Frida raised her eyebrows. "Aha. And what does a yield sign mean?"

"Caution." Sarah got goosebumps suddenly. "Is this a warning about danger?"

"Possibly. Though I think we all have to use caution at every point in our lives. Complacency is what gets us killed." Frida paused, gazing at the cards. "Maybe someone you love needs some caution, some help along the way? Just a suggestion, but not a direct interpretation. Again, this is all up to you."

An image of Dismas, tall and disturbing in his camouflage, flashed into Sarah's mind. She got a creepy feeling in her stomach.

"Now, my next client is about to come, so I have to wrap this up. But take the book. And please, tell

Michael Howler hello for me. I really do miss him." Frida smiled kindly as she guided Sarah to the door, giving Addie one final pet.

Sarah and Addie trudged away from the house. "I have a lot to think about," Sarah said.

"I smell the fox nearby. The fox is always nearby, always watching you," Addie informed her.

"Can you help me catch up to it?" Sarah asked.

Addie shook her head. *"The fox is too fast for me. You have to do it."*

Sarah nodded and sighed. "Of course."

CHAPTER SEVEN

AT THE CONCLUSION OF HER MEETING WITH FRIDA, Sarah met up with Eli, and the two began to search for other people's missing good luck charms. Eli mentioned that two people had come into the station that day to report stolen family heirlooms, so they went to see Chris first.

Chris Graylock was of Abenaki descent and owned a small vegetable and bean farm outside of town. His family had farmed the land for generations, so far back that Chris was not quite sure when they had first settled the piece of property.

Chris was standing outside, drying his oil-stained hands on a rag. He had been working on fixing up his small tractor for the summer, which had broken down. "Hi, Officer Eli." He greeted Sarah with a nod. "Are you guys here about my canoe?"

"You said in your report a painted canoe was stolen," Eli said. "Can you describe your painted canoe?"

"It's been in my family for years. It had an eagle, wolf, fox, and bear on it. My ancestors had put it over there on the banks of the small pond next to the fields for good luck to watch over the crops. We haven't had a case of powdery mildew or anything else the entire time we've lived here. Now the canoe is missing, and guess what? My bean sprouts are toast." Chris looked heavily at the long rows of wilted bean plant seedlings behind his modest house.

"Can't you plant more?" Eli asked, naïve about farming.

"Sure I could! But along with the beans, the sister crops of corn and squash are failing, too," Chris explained. "I worry the whole harvest will be ruined. At this rate, if I plant more, they will be ripening too late in the season, when it starts turning cold. This is bad, very bad."

"Do you have any idea who might have taken the canoe?" Sarah prodded.

Chris vehemently shook his head. "No one I know of. It's been a prized possession in my family for generations, and I hoped to keep it that way." He suddenly looked crestfallen. "I can't believe I'm the first one in the family to lose it."

"You said it's worth a lot?" Eli asked.

Chris nodded slowly. "My grandfather had it appraised once by a Native American collector. It was worth ten thousand in the early eighties, so . . ."

"Sounds like a simple robbery," Eli concluded, flipping the pad he was taking notes on shut. "Someone saw an easy way to make a nice tidy fortune. Relatively untraceable, too, without any kind of serial number on it."

"Don't blame yourself," Sarah attempted to console Chris. But her words seemed to have little effect on his depressed mood.

"We'll look into it and do what we can. We'll check the next big Native artifact auction," Eli promised.

Chris nodded and thanked them before dejectedly turning to his tractor.

"Poor guy. See? Another good luck charm gone and more bad luck," Sarah told Eli as they walked back to Eli's car.

"I doubt it has anything to do with luck, Sarah, and more to do with money," Eli replied.

Next, they located Landon Ursa, who worked in a small café in the town square. He also had filed a police report that day for the loss of a silver brooch that his grandmother had given him many years before.

"I wouldn't say it's a good luck charm," the huge bear of a man said as he peeled potatoes for the night's homemade French fries. "But it comforts me, you know? It puts me in a frame of mind to make good choices and form my own luck. That was the strength my grandma wanted me to have when she gave it to me. She wanted me to remember her by it always and draw courage from it." His eyes grew misty.

"Was it valuable?" Eli asked. "Pure silver?"

He shrugged. "Probably not worth that much. I don't know."

"Where did you lose it?" Sarah asked.

"I was at batting practice. You know I play on the town's baseball league. Anyway, when I went to get my duffel bag and change after practice, it was gone. I always leave it pinned to that bag. It's like an athlete's lucky shoes or something," he explained.

"And did your luck seem to take a turn for the worse?" Sarah went on.

"Funny you mention that. I actually threw my back out right after it went missing. I'll be out of the games for weeks now, and I'm their star player. I'm no old man; I'm only twenty-five! I've never had back problems in my life. And to make matters worse, my car won't start now. Who knows how much this will set me back. I was trying to save up to get a place with my girlfriend." Landon sighed heavily. "I know it seems silly, but it all started when I lost that brooch."

Eli and Sarah thanked Landon for his time. He

smiled grimly and told them he hoped that they would find his brooch, at least for his grandmother's sake. As they walked away, Eli finally conceded to Sarah, "Something funky *is* going on in this town."

Their final visit was to Harriet. Sarah groaned as they approached her lopsided hut with smoke curling out of its chimney. "I guarantee you this is going to be weird," she told Eli.

Edgar announced their arrival before they could even knock, flapping his wings violently and squawking at the top of his lungs, *"That attorney with the red hair is here! And her boy toy!"*

Harriet came to the door, a smelly steam clouding out around her into the cool April air. She squinted at them, clearly wondering why they had stopped by.

"Can we come in for a second and talk to you about your lucky bauble?" Eli began.

"My lucky bauble, eh? I'm in the middle of making a potion." She glanced behind her to ascertain it was boiling properly. "I don't advise guests to stand near it. It has . . . effects."

"Is there somewhere else we can sit?" Sarah asked.

Harriet ushered them around the back of her hut, where she had arranged a few rickety chairs around an earthen hearth. "My bread is just cooling. Would you like some?" She pulled out a wooden tray of green bread.

Eli and Sarah exchanged repulsed looks before politely declining.

"Suit yourselves! This is made from the finest cave slime, to bring back youthful rejuvenation and heart health." Harriet picked a hunk off of the loaf and popped it into her mouth, making exaggerated sounds of enjoyment.

"Hmmm." Eli leaned forward in his seat and pressed the tips of his fingers together into a tent. "Can you please tell us more about your lucky bauble?"

"My enameled newt eye. Just plain disappeared," Harriet answered.

Sarah and Eli exchanged looks. "Enameled newt eye? That's the bauble?" Eli confirmed, now scribbling on his notepad.

Harriet nodded and shrugged, as if owning an enameled newt eye was the most natural thing in the world.

"When did it disappear?" Sarah asked.

"Geez, Sarah, if I knew that, then I'd probably have it." Harriet chuckled.

Sarah shook her head. "Then let's try this. When did you last have it?"

Harriet leaned forward to peer at Sarah. Sarah realized her eyes were almost completely obfuscated by cataracts, and she had no idea how Harriet saw as well as she did.

"If you can't tell, I'm blind as a bat. I carry that newt eye with me to see for me. But the other morning, I woke up blind, and haven't been able to find it since," she related. Then she cackled as she settled back into her chair, the wood creaking under her. "A bit hard to search for things when you can't see!"

"Harriet," Sarah said compassionately, reaching for Harriet's arm. "I think there are surgeries that can remove those cataracts. Glasses and prescriptions. Why don't you see an eye doctor?"

"*No doctors!*" Edgar squawked.

Harriet merely waved her hand while grinning mischievously. "I would scare the whole staff out of the building if I arrived. Besides, witches don't use doctors; we use our own magic. Haven't you heard the term 'witch doctor'?"

"There is nothing wrong with using a doctor when something is truly wrong," Eli gently cajoled her.

"I like my newt eye, thank you very much. It's become an old friend to me. Sleeps under my pillow and whispers things from the caves that make me happy."

Sarah had to suppress a shudder. Harriet's affinity for cave exploration had become known to her last fall, when she also found herself trapped in the caves under Mount Katribus.

"Are you two here to find it or what?" Harriet

squinted at them, and Sarah wondered how poor her vision was.

"There's been a string of related thefts throughout town, and we are definitely working to get to the bottom of this," Eli assured her.

"Okay. Just no need for magical lightsaber fighting with Madras this time." Harriet cackled and winked at Sarah. "This isn't Madras's doing."

Sarah gaped at her, wondering how she knew about last fall's debacle on the mountaintop, and also in surprise that she was a *Star Wars* fan. Harriet was certainly an odd woman, and Sarah was beginning to develop a keen curiosity for her other secrets.

"How do you know Madras isn't here?" Sarah inquired. "Have you seen her in the caves, perhaps?"

"No, the cave creatures tell me that she is long gone. And I don't feel her," Harriet replied. Then she smirked. "Can't you, too, being her little niece?"

Sarah sighed. "No, I don't feel her, either. I was just checking to see if you had any information I didn't."

"I'm sure I have lots of information you don't. Whether or not you would be interested in it is a different story." Harriet's eyes twinkled despite their milky coating of cataracts.

Sarah didn't know what to say. She and Eli thanked Harriet and left.

"That's weird. Who would want to take her sight? I really feel whoever is doing this is working to create trouble in the town. Stealing eyes, stealing good luck, ruining crops. Something is definitely going on, and it seems dark," Sarah mused. Then she blanched. "I really pray there won't be another murder!"

Eli put his arm around her and pulled her close. "I sure hope so, too," he said bleakly. "I hate when lives are lost to evil."

Their final stop was Susan Lake's office. Sarah had urged Eli to ask her some questions, since she had been Frida's last client the day the cards went missing. Susan Lake was rapidly typing on her laptop, a mug of tea near her hand. She smiled when they entered and shut her laptop lid. "What a pleasure to see you two! Out for a little stroll? It sure is a nice day." She glanced out the window at the pleasant weather.

"Actually, this is a business visit," Eli said apologetically.

"Uh-oh. What's the matter?" Susan Lake pressed her lips in a thin line as she awaited whatever the pair had to say.

"Were you at Frida Pecto's parlor four days ago?" Sarah asked.

Susan Lake looked taken aback, then sheepish. "Wow, I thought Frida protected our confidentiality.

I'm certainly never going to her again." She shook her head, clearly embarrassed.

"Frida just told us because we asked," Sarah assured her. "She didn't share anything about your visit or reading."

"Don't be embarrassed," Eli said gently, placing a hand on her shoulder. "You're not in trouble. We just wanted to confirm Frida's story."

"Yes, I was." Susan folded her hands on top of her laptop. "I've lived here all of my life, and I normally don't mess with the magic stuff—or even care about it. But you have to admit, living in Witchland, it seeps into you. It almost becomes normal to go get your fortune read." She shook her head. "I just needed some guidance, some clarity, on where to go with my life now that I will be retiring and handing off my interim position."

"Did Frida perform an animal spirit team reading on you?" Sarah inquired.

"She did." Susan Lake nodded, still seeming uncomfortable after her confession to using Frida's services. "What is this regarding, if I may ask?"

"Sure. When you left, Frida's animal oracle cards were stolen," Sarah explained.

Susan scoffed. "And you think I did it?"

"No, no, we were just wondering if you saw anyone suspicious?" Eli asked.

"Suspicious?" Susan shrugged. "Um, only person I saw was Malorie. She stopped me at the door and said hello."

"Malorie?" Sarah noticed Eli scribbling something on his notepad. "Did Malorie go inside with you at all?"

"No." Susan shrugged. "Not that I saw."

"Thanks for your time." Sarah stood, and Eli followed. They said goodbye to Susan, who was staring after them perplexedly.

"Bye," Susan said, sounding puzzled.

"I think we need to investigate Malorie for sure," Sarah said. "Maybe she can shapeshift or turn invisible, hence why no one saw her go inside."

"Remember, that's just a theory that Malorie stole the cards. We need to gather more evidence first," Eli said.

"I know. I'll go home and meditate on all of this and come up with a list of other likely suspects," Sarah said.

CHAPTER EIGHT

A BEAUTIFUL DUSK WITH COLORS OF PINK, BLUE, and gray descended over Witchland. The birds settled into the dark trees, ruffling their feathers, gently cheeping to each other, their babies safely nestled in nests. An owl flew across Sarah's yard, beginning his nightly hunt, and the bats swooped out of the church steeple where they slept all day long.

Sarah sat on the swing on the tiny porch in front of her house, a mug of warm tea between her hands, reflecting on the missing good luck charms. Who would want to steal charms, some of which were worthless to everyone but their owners? What was this person—or thing—trying to accomplish? It seemed like mayhem was the only goal this thief had in mind.

Then her mouth dropped open as a revelation occurred to her. Maybe this thief was not trying to cause bad luck; maybe whoever it was needed some good luck. She hastily ran inside to grab a notepad and jot down the names of everyone she could think of who needed to steal good luck. Obviously, there was Malorie, first on the list. But she also added Roger Miller and, after some hesitation, Hua. Though she didn't actually suspect Hua, she wanted to be fair to everyone and investigate all of the candidates equally. It occurred to her that Oscar Reedy might also need luck in order to prevent the town's acquisition of the extra forest so that he could continue hosting hunters on the public land.

Sarah paused, chewing the pen cap. She could not think of anyone else who might need luck. So why did she keep thinking of the fox? The fox was becoming her obsession of sorts.

An idea popped into her head, and she wrote, "Background check?" over Malorie's name. No one knew much about the mysterious business owner who had simply appeared in Witchland a few years ago.

Sarah texted Eli, "I have a hunch about the charms. Let's look into Roger, Malorie, and Oscar. And Hua, just to be fair."

"Sure thing," he responded. "Want to go with me to question them tomorrow?"

"Sure," she wrote back.

Then she set her phone down, taking in the gathering darkness. She smiled down at Addie and Kelvin, cuddled together by her feet, sound asleep. Addie's legs kicked slightly in rhythm to whatever dream she was having. Kelvin was never truly asleep, always on the lookout for danger, as any wild animal would be, but a slight smile played on his thick black lips as he kept one paw on Addie's shoulder. Sarah missed Eli on these nights when they didn't stay together, and she had to remind herself not to be too codependent. She just couldn't believe that she had managed to end up with someone whom she couldn't get enough of. When she thought of Eli, she still got butterflies, and she realized that she was absolutely crazy about him.

Pink, she thought, her mind turning to her interesting reading with Frida. *Love. I . . . love Eli!*

But did he love her? She was pretty sure he did, but her divorce now made it hard to trust that anyone loved her fully. She liked how things were; she liked taking it slowly, enjoying each day as it came, not rushing anything and letting it all happen organically.

The next morning, Eli knocked on Sarah's door, bearing coffee and crullers from Javacadabra. The two trekked off toward the hunting lodge, determined to confront the first and most menacing person on Sarah's short list.

Just as they approached the tree line of the woods, the fox appeared. She paused to look at Sarah, her black eyes dancing with mirth. A smirk played on her lips.

"Hey, babe, can you wait a sec?" Sarah handed Eli her coffee and pastry and told Addie to wait.

"*You go ahead,*" Addie said. "*This is your time with the fox, not mine.*"

Sarah took off after the fox. She did not chase it, but rather followed it with slow, deliberate steps.

The fox waited until Sarah was a yard away before trotting off into the trees. Sarah followed it for a while, twigs and pine needles snapping under her shoes, until they were out of Eli's earshot.

"*Tell me, how are you doing?*" the fox asked facetiously. It sat in a small hollow between two tree roots, its red tail curled neatly around its front legs, like a cat. But its face was sharp and distinctly dog-like as it surveyed Sarah, memorizing her features.

"You're talking to me," Sarah said, stunned.

The fox let out a short bark of a laugh. "*Honey, I'm all yours if you can outsmart the good-luck thief!*"

"What can you tell me about this thief?" Sarah inquired.

"*That's not outsmarting it if I give you all the*

answers, now is it? You have to prove yourself to me. Show me you are worth my kind as your spirit animals." The fox licked its chops, clearly relishing the moment.

Sarah shook her head. "Well . . . watch out for Oscar. He's back and hunting again."

The fox laughed again. *"He's no more of a threat than a toddler with a toy gun."*

Sarah snorted. "How can you say that after what he did before? He has fox heads mounted all over the lodge."

"Maybe it's you who is afraid of him, because I'm not," the fox replied smugly. Then the fox stood up and bounded off into the woods, making it clear that Sarah could not chase it.

Sarah headed back to Eli and Addie. Eli looked puzzled as he handed her breakfast back. "Now it's foxes, not wolves?" he asked, only half joking.

Sarah groaned. "I am supposed to get to know this fox. It's possibly going to be one of my animal spirit guides. But I honestly don't care for it! It's so smart-alecky and rude. And it isn't very helpful. It acts like I have to impress it."

"I hate the way it smells and that I can't ever catch it," Addie lamented.

Eli nodded thoughtfully. "Maybe you don't actually need to impress it? The point of gaining the fox as your guide is to prove something to yourself, not the fox."

Sarah had never thought of that before. Her heart swelled with appreciation for Eli as she pecked his cheek. "Perhaps it's a part of myself I must unlock to become more like Lativia." Sarah then thought of the other two animals that had not revealed themselves to Frida, or to her, yet.

"Michael, what do you think?" she asked the air, wondering if she could summon him.

"You chose one wise man," Michael's voice floated into her mind.

They finally reached the lodge. Oscar was already leaving, armed and camouflaged. He snarled with annoyance when he saw them approaching. Addie raised her hackles and growled, and he curled his lip at her, an obvious show of aggression. Sarah bristled with dislike for the man standing before her.

"What the hell do you two want? I've done nothing wrong," he snapped.

"We just have a few questions about some items that have gone missing around town," Eli began, showing his badge, even though Oscar knew fully well who he was. "We would appreciate your cooperation."

"Missing items? You're calling me a thief? I work for my rewards." Oscar was turning red, his nostrils flaring.

"Would you happen to know anything about a painted Abenaki canoe? Worth thousands?" Sarah piped up.

"No." He snorted. "Do I look like I'm into collecting canoes? Geez." He shouldered his heavy bow and arrow.

"What are you hunting today, Oscar?" Eli pressed.

"Nothing that I'm not allowed to," he shot back. "Yeah, I looked into the laws, and there is no law against hunting and trapping red foxes in New Hampshire. That tells me your girlfriend here is full of nonsense. Endangered species, ha!" He snorted derisively. "Actually, honey, there's no bag limit. At all."

"They may not be endangered, but they're rare in these woods," Sarah snapped. "You're harming an entire ecosystem by hunting them. Why don't you focus on hunting foxes in places where they're common? Leave this ecosystem alone."

Oscar shook his head. "What you people fail to understand is that we humans dominate this ecosystem. We are apex predators. We need meat to survive." He slammed down the trunk of his Range Rover and began to make his way to the driver's seat.

"Don't walk away while I'm talking to you," Eli shouted.

"We're done here," Oscar tossed over his shoulder. "I'm an honest man and an honest business owner. You can follow me, ask people about me, whatever you want. You got nothing on me. Now excuse me, I have traps to set."

Sarah cringed. "Traps seem even crueler than guns," she muttered to Eli.

Eli gritted his teeth. "But sadly, they're not illegal."

"Oscar, wait," Sarah said.

Oscar turned and surveyed her expectantly.

"I just really need to apologize for coming off so coarse the other day. I really didn't mean to insult you or to get off on the wrong foot with you. I want us to be able to work together," Sarah said.

Oscar was quiet for a moment before saying, "To tell you the truth, of course I want that, too. May I ask why you started acting hostile toward me? And why you're up here accusing me of being a thief?"

"I . . . it's hard to explain. I just heard a . . . a rumor that you were harming animals in the forest, and I had to intervene," Sarah explained.

"A rumor? Who on earth told you that?" Oscar barked.

Sarah cringed. *Great, now I have to make something up! Who knows if he believes in the Leekins?*

But before she could come up with a lie, Oscar added, "This doesn't have anything to do with our little forest friends, the Leekins, does it?"

Sarah let out a laugh of relief. "You know about the Leekins!"

"Miss Spellwood, you can't spend as much time in the forest as I do and not know about the Leekins. The little faeries are always buzzing in my ear and misplacing my hunting knives. They don't like me, and I guess I can see why, but they should know that hunting is not evil in and of itself. In fact, it is necessary to keep some animal populations balanced. We once had an overabundance of deer; I managed to keep that down with my guide work," Oscar explained.

Sarah sighed. "I'm glad you won't think I'm crazy then. Flora McLeafy told me you were back, and she seemed distraught. And it reminded me so much of Dismas that my trauma took over. You know that Dismas tried to kill both my dog and me, right?"

Oscar cleared his throat. "I understand, and no hard feelings, Miss Spellwood. I'm not like Dismas, though. And actually, I came back here to shut down my hunting lodge and sell it because I don't want to host any more people like Dismas. I don't want to be implicated in crimes and poaching. I have too much honor."

"Thank you for that," Sarah said. "Perhaps instead of shutting this place down, you could turn it into a different type of establishment? A glamping lodge, for instance?"

"Yeah, well, my whole plan was to sell it. Not into the 'glamorous camping' thing—not my style. But if that crackpot Roger Miller gets elected as mayor, I'll lose all my hunting grounds and the lodge won't be worth anything. I might as well just make it my retirement home. Maybe Airbnb some of the rooms or something the way Malorie does. She's done well for herself." He sounded disgruntled.

Sarah nodded, appreciating his feelings and how there were always two sides to everything. Now the cons to Roger Miller's plan were apparent, and she understood why so many small business owners opposed it. "I'm sorry to hear that. I hope maybe we can reach some sort of compromise on the forest. I don't want you to lose your livelihood."

"My livelihood won't be ruined. I have another establishment up in Maine. But it will be a significant loss in income, that's for sure." He grunted. "Anyway, why do you think I'm behind the missing objects? I'm not a thief!"

"The objects missing are all good luck charms or things people need," Sarah explained. "I think someone might need luck, so they're stealing items. That did make you a bit of a suspect, to be honest."

"I didn't do it, but I want to thank you for being a straight shooter, Miss Spellwood."

"You can call me Sarah." She chuckled. "Miss

Spellwood makes me feel like a southern belle getting ready for a debutante ball."

He laughed. "In that case, Sarah, you have a good day now."

"Bye." Sarah waved, feeling relieved.

"*That must feel good,*" Addie said happily. She hated conflict.

"*It sure did,*" Sarah said. "*Maybe he can be an ally for us.*"

Eli and Sarah then moved on, in search of Roger. They soon found him surveying the land at the edge of the woods he wanted to acquire.

"Hi, Roger," Sarah called pleasantly.

He paused, glancing up at them. Then he shook Sarah's and Eli's hands. "Sorry, guys, I'm trying to get a map updated for my conference at the town hall today." He appeared flustered, and sweat glistened on his neck, which was slightly sunburned. With an agitated movement, he swatted at a deerfly that landed on his bicep, poised to bite. "These dang flies today!"

"We just had some questions for you," Eli began.

"There's another one!" Roger swatted at his calf, left bare by his khaki shorts.

"Have you seen a painted Native American canoe? Or a silver brooch?" Eli ventured.

"Or a potion vial? Or a horseshoe?" Sarah asked.

Roger paused, looking at them with confusion

written all over his face. "Huh?" he finally asked. "What, a Native American canoe?"

Sarah and Eli glanced at each other. It was clear Roger was not their guy.

"Thanks anyway," Eli finally said, waving as they turned away.

"Uh-huh." Roger watched them leave, confusion still on his face, before turning back to his work.

"By the way . . ." Eli turned on his heel.

"Yeah?" Roger looked up. He started to appear annoyed.

"How do you plan to buy all of this land?"

"Uh . . ." Roger scratched his head. "That's what I'm working on right now."

"Thank you." Eli waved again, and he and Sarah left Roger.

"Maybe you're right," Sarah admitted sheepishly. "He's pretty naïve."

"He's a great guy, with a great idea," Eli acknowledged, "but with no action plan, he is as good as useless."

As Eli and Sarah walked to the next suspect in line for questioning, Eli began to talk about the election again.

He kept mentioning how much he liked Malorie and how bad Roger was.

"I think Roger would be a fantastic candidate, with a bit of help and guidance," Sarah said.

Eli laughed patronizingly. "Sarah, you always mean well, but electing him would be naïve."

Sarah bristled. There was that condescending tone again. "You know, I don't really appreciate how you just spoke to me." In her marriage, she had often ignored her feelings, too scared of confrontation to ever reveal how hurt she felt. She wasn't going to do that anymore. A true relationship was supposed to be based on communication, trust, and respect.

Eli surprised her when he stopped and clutched her waist, pulling her into him. "Wow, I'm sorry. I had no idea that's how I made you feel."

Sarah softened into his firm chest and touched his cheek. "I know you didn't mean it. But it's how I felt. I really need to feel that we're equals and we're in this together, not that you're the man and I'm the woman. That's not how I work in relationships."

"Of course not. That's not how I work, either." Eli sighed. "I think being a cop makes me get a little too authoritative . . . out of habit. If I ever do that with you again, please, let me know right away. I'll do anything to fix it." He buried his face into Sarah's hair, holding her close.

"Eli?" she said, finally pulling away slightly, placing her hands squarely on his chest.

"Hm?" He gazed down at her, his eyes soft and full of love.

"I love you." The words poured out of her before she could overthink them.

Eli's face lit up with joy. "I love you, too, Sarah Spellwood."

Addie sighed happily, watching her favorite person being swept off her feet.

Following this, they reached the large house with the barn converted into a greenhouse in the back. Hua was working in the garden, lovingly laboring over her plants. She straightened and dusted the dirt off of her gardening gloves when Eli and Sarah approached.

"Hi, Hua," Sarah said brightly.

"Hi, Sarah, Eli," Hua responded warmly. "I sense the two of you are sleuthing!" She bent forward to scratch Addie behind the ears.

"We are, actually." Sarah laughed. "You know us."

"Is there anything I can help you with?" Hua asked.

"Just so you know, you're not under suspicion," Eli began. "But we do wonder if you might know anything about the good luck charms that have been going missing."

"Good luck charms are missing?" Margaret spoke

up, approaching behind them with a large water jug. "That doesn't sound good."

Sarah caught the couple up on the thefts occurring around the town and the bad luck that had befallen each of the victims. The two witches exchanged worried looks. "I don't know anything about this, but it doesn't sound good at all. Your hunch that it might have to do with the mayoral election is concerning and probably right," Hua finally said.

"I hope it isn't true, and I hope it has nothing to do with Madras," Sarah said. "Though Harriet swears there is no sign of Madras in the caves under the town. It would seem she is truly gone."

"That's good, though you know Madras is a crafty one who can hide in plain sight," Margaret said.

"Do you guys know anything about Malorie? She's actually my prime suspect at this time," Sarah asked.

The two witches exchanged shrugs. "She just seemed to materialize out of thin air. She is always working on her businesses, keeping to herself. We really don't know her well," Margaret finally answered.

"Come to think of it, I can't believe how little I do know about her," Hua added. "This is a small town, and we usually know everything about each other. It's weird that she has stayed relatively under the radar for the past few years, especially as a newcomer. There was a lot of curiosity about her when she first arrived, but it has faded, since she's given no one any gossip fodder."

Sarah nodded with concern, remembering how much curiosity had surrounded her own arrival. Everyone had known everything about her, even before she had arrived, thanks to Michael's bragging about his prodigious friend and former law student. It did seem suspicious that Malorie was keenly enigmatic.

"Does she have any friends or close associates?" Eli asked.

"No one I know of. She talks to people, but no one I would call a friend. And she works alone," Margaret replied.

"Thank you both," Sarah said graciously. "That helps more than you know."

"Really? I'm glad to help." Hua beamed.

"Of course. It shows me where to point my investigative efforts." Sarah smiled. She hugged both Margaret and Hua and promised to come by for dinner and herbal magic lessons soon. As she walked away, she told Eli that she didn't suspect Hua was capable of stealing anything, and he vehemently agreed.

Soon after, Eli and Sarah located Malorie cleaning out one of her cabins for an upcoming guest. It appeared that the weekend was about to be a busy one for Witchland with lots of visitors from all over the place.

"Hello!" she crowed when she saw them, her wry face lighting up with enthusiasm. "Are you looking for a honeymoon suite? I have just the cabin for you." She produced a brochure from the sheath in her leather satchel, which she apparently carried around with her everywhere.

Eli and Sarah exchanged glances. Though they were both still glowing from the exchange of "I love you" in the woods, they weren't quite sure why Malorie thought they needed a honeymoon suite in the very town where they both lived. "We live here," Eli said with an awkward chuckle.

"But you've never seen this town from the suite's bay window," Malorie protested suavely. She began to show off the shiny photos of what appeared to be a truly romantic, quaint suite with a huge four-post bed. "A dozen chocolate-dipped strawberries waiting for you on the bed, champagne on ice, a heart-shaped Jacuzzi hot tub, a dozen different bath salts to choose from, and satin sheets," she went on. "Isn't it too bad that it's not Valentine's Day?"

"Maybe next Valentine's Day," Eli said, pushing her brochure away.

"Maybe you'd prefer one of my other cabins.

Simplicity and rustic living, right in your own backyard!" Malorie pushed on.

"That sounds wonderful, but we're not looking for a place to stay. We have simple and rustic in our own homes," Sarah said.

Eli added, "We just have a few questions for you."

"Shoot!" Malorie tucked her brochures back into her satchel, finally getting the hint that her pushy sales tactics were unwelcome at the moment.

When Eli began to ask her about the charms, she looked taken aback. Then she laughed. "These things don't seem to have much value, do they?"

"The canoe is worth thousands," Sarah volunteered.

Malorie pursed her lips. "But the other thefts? They seem quite random, if you ask me."

"We think it has something to do with luck," Sarah ventured. "They're good luck tokens, for the owners anyway."

Malorie laughed out loud. "If someone's stealing and selling good luck charms, I'm buying! I need all the luck I can get with this election coming up." Then she sobered when she saw the serious expressions on Eli's and Sarah's faces. "I know nothing about these good luck charms, guys. Sorry I can't be of more help."

"Thank you," they both said.

As they began to walk out of the cabin, Malorie

added, "Stealing good luck charms seems like a desperate measure. It had better be worth it, because I wouldn't dare mess with others' good luck charms—especially not in this town full of witches! Who knows what kinds of powerful enemies that could make? Whoever is doing it is either a fool . . . or very clever indeed."

Sarah paused. Malorie's words rang with truth. Who would gain anything by stealing the good luck charms of others? Perhaps her theory about someone trying to attract good luck was wrong. After all, none of her suspects seemed particularly guilty. "Thanks," she told Malorie.

Malorie nodded as she turned back to her cleaning.

"I guess we should let this go for now," Eli urged Sarah as they trudged toward the town square. "I'll keep an eye out for that canoe, and the other items, but this case seems rather closed to me right now."

"Yeah," said Sarah, though she had a sense that this case was not closed. Michael's words about solving it alone echoed in her mind.

After kissing Eli goodbye, Sarah returned to the house. She sat at her desk and called to Michael. "Michael! Do you want to join me in looking into Malorie?"

Michael's presence filled the room and bathed Sarah in warmth, while also raising the hairs along her neck and arms. "I missed working together," he said enthusiastically. "Let's start with a simple social media search into Malorie's background."

For the next several hours, Sarah used her lawyer's resources to conduct a full background check on Malorie. By the end, her spine tingled. There was absolutely no trace of this woman before she moved to Witchland. Clearly, she had changed her name, but Sarah could not locate any documentation of that change. She texted Eli for a license plate number, and he reported that Malorie did not even own a car. The next day, when they checked deeds to learn what information Malorie had provided the banks to purchase all of her properties, they discovered that she had purchased them all with cash directly from the owners, under "Malorie Vulpes."

"Is it just me, or is this creepy?" Sarah asked Eli with a shallow laugh.

"Definitely. This is literally a person without a trace." Eli shook his head. "We have no idea who her family is or where she came from. I think we should question her again."

"Right? Even if she's not stealing the items, it disturbs me to have someone running for mayor who has an unknown background. No history, no employer references, nobody to indicate her character." Sarah groaned. "We really should run background checks on our mayoral candidates from now on because elections are tomorrow! This is insane."

Eli agreed.

"I think it's time I went undercover," Sarah decided. "I have to go invisible and follow Malorie for a day. See what she does, where she goes."

Addie barked in excitement. She loved her camouflaged sleuthing adventures with Sarah.

After leaving Eli, Sarah camouflaged herself and Addie with a spell that made her blend in with her surroundings. Then she jogged to the bed and breakfast, where Malorie lived on the bottom floor.

As soon as she entered the establishment, she found Malorie in the orange-tiled kitchen. There was a couple staying, and she was dipping strawberries in white chocolate for them. She hummed a little tune and tapped her foot in rhythm. She seemed to freeze and glance around in confusion the minute Sarah entered the room, and Sarah feared that her cover was blown. Perhaps Malorie had powers? Could she be a plant from Madras?

Malorie seemed to look right at her. But then her face turned blank once again, and she resumed her task. Shortly after, she began to assemble the strawberries on a special golden tray shaped like a heart.

For the next several hours, Addie and Sarah observed Malorie without excitement. She seemed to be an ordinary person, working hard at her business. While she was folding towels for the bathroom, Sarah slipped downstairs to Malorie's office and opened her books. The books looked normal, and Sarah couldn't find a single document demonstrating Malorie's identity.

"This is weird, Addie. Who is this person? And why doesn't she have anything—a social security card, a birth certificate, even a driver's license?" Sarah shook her head.

Just then, Addie let out a bark. Sarah jumped. *"Addie! Malorie will hear you!"* she hissed.

"Sorry! But look!" Addie was pointing toward the window with her snout.

Sarah looked out the glass and realized the fox was standing there, staring back at her with angry black eyes. Sarah set down the book she was combing through and ran outside. *"Hey! Wait! Come back!"* she called after the animal as it loped away.

The fox stopped and sat at the tree line, curling its tail neatly around its body. *"It's a pity you can't see what's right in front of you, and instead you have to snoop!"* it said.

Sarah paused. *"I'm doing it for the good of this town. You know that I took a vow to protect the woods."*

"Maybe consider a more straightforward method?" The fox then took off into the trees.

Sarah's shoulders slumped. "*This is discouraging. I can't seem to make this fox happy! What she has to tell me had better be important.*"

Addie merely barked again, and Sarah admonished her for blowing their cover. Scared that perhaps Maloric was looking out the window at them, Sarah slipped into the trees to regain her and Addie's camouflage. When they reentered the house, they found Malorie sitting on the stairs, on the phone and apparently unperturbed by Addie's bark in her office. They followed her for the rest of the day until she went to sleep, then they waited outside her door in case she ever snuck out, but she did nothing suspicious at all.

CHAPTER NINE

With the bustle of the first warm spring weekend behind them, everyone assembled at the school gymnasium on Monday morning to cast their ballots for town mayor. The simple gymnasium had been converted into a polling place, with Susan Lake overseeing the ballot counting. Everyone gathered into two neat lines, shuffling forward as the person ahead finished voting.

"Who do you think is going to win?" Hua asked Sarah anxiously, rubbing her hands together. After many months of hard work, she was exhausted, with deep bags under her eyes.

"Hopefully you!" Sarah said, trying her best to sound sincere. Honestly, she had no idea who she wanted to win. Malorie seemed like a no now that she knew about her lack of background; Roger was too vapid with his plans; and Hua had no real plans, at least nothing substantial, anyway. Witchland's fate seemed precarious, and the tension running through the mass of voters reflected that.

Sarah, Daisy, Hua, and Margaret froze when they heard the sound of shouting ahead. An angry, red-faced man had started berating another man, "How dare you? You're going to be the downfall of this town!"

"Calm down, Carl!" his wife cried, clearly humiliated as she tugged on his sleeve.

"Don't tell me to calm down!" he roared. "This town is broke as it is! And you want to put it in the hands of a bleeding-heart tree hugger?"

Sarah wrapped her arms around herself. It bothered her to see this kind of sentiment and division in Witchland, a town known for its environmental fervor and peace. Good thing the tourists were gone or they would never come back, thinking this place was full of violent, angry folk!

"Frankly, I just want to get out of here," Daisy muttered into Sarah's ear. "I want to get back to my shop."

"Why, hello, dear!" Sarah turned at the sound of Frida's voice. Frida stood there, overdressed as usual, her arms outstretched for a hug.

"Oh." Sarah laughed awkwardly, accepting Frida's embrace.

"Daisy," Frida said with cold civility, breaking away from Sarah.

"Frida," Daisy replied stiffly.

"Did I tell you that Daisy and I went to college together? And we both learned about Spellwood magic from the same woman, Crystal Ernestine MacBeth," Frida told Sarah. "She was our hospitality professor and knew we both had gifts."

"Oh?" Sarah glanced at Daisy, surprised to hear this bit of history.

"Oh, yes. Daisy was quite the stellar student," Frida went on.

"When you weren't busy overshadowing me and showing off," Daisy replied, an unpleasantly tight expression on her face. Sarah had never seen Daisy so tense.

"Ha ha, of course, you were always too distracted by boys to pay much attention," Frida shot back. "Old Mrs. MacBeth was always at her wits' end with you!"

"Frida, you really ought to come by our greenhouse," Margaret spoke up, trying to defuse the icy tension mounting between the two witches. "We don't see you enough, and we would love to hear some of your thoughts on some new plants we have acquired for our collection."

"I would be delighted!" Frida cried, clapping her hands. "I had better get back to my place in line, as people are starting to grumble."

As Frida bustled away, Sarah turned to Daisy. "Why isn't Frida in our coven?" she inquired.

"Thank the heavens she isn't!" Daisy scoffed.

"We witches have to band together," Hua reminded Daisy gently. "Leaving someone out leaves us vulnerable."

"She's just a commercialized fake Gypsy, not a real witch," Daisy replied. "We really aren't any more or less vulnerable without her!"

"I found her reading on me to be quite telling," Sarah volunteered.

Daisy shot her a betrayed look before turning to face ahead and falling silent.

"And you are the one who told me sisters must band together. We could use someone in our coven who has psychic powers," Sarah pressed on.

"Especially since we've been blindsided by evil in this town more than once! She's sensitive, and she could be a real asset to our efforts," Margaret added.

Daisy refused to reply, but Sarah could see the tension in her shoulders dissipate slightly.

"She used to be an initiate of our coven," Hua recalled. "But then that drama with Earl . . ."

"There was no drama with Earl," Daisy spoke up, a

slight quiver in her voice. "He wanted to move on, and I let him. You love something, you let it go. If it is meant to be, he will come back. Only Earl never came back to me."

"Who was Earl?" Sarah asked, curious about this man who managed to capture the hearts of two witches. In her mind, she tried to imagine him, an enigmatic and devilishly handsome Brad Pitt lookalike but with black hair and a wizard's cape.

"He was the only warlock to join our coven, besides Michael," Margaret explained. "A very powerful man. Also a great storyteller."

"He was really funny," Hua reminisced.

"He left not long after we got here from Manhattan," Margaret went on. "Decided he had bigger and better things to do in Wales."

"A mythical quest for dragons," Daisy scoffed, finally turning back to face Sarah.

"Wait, dragons?" Sarah had thought nothing could surprise her anymore since her introduction to the world of magic, but dragons? "Dragons are real?"

"There is no firsthand evidence," Margaret said firmly. "Some hearsay, sure, but no photographs, videos, recordings that are reliable. Dragons are a bit like Sasquatch, an elusive legend with no solid evidence. The dragon craze seemed to die down in the Middle Ages, anyway."

"Now only a few overzealous explorers seek them . . . like Earl," Daisy added. "Leave it to men to become infatuated with fantasy creatures! If you want my opinion, dragons are just old dinosaur bones that peasants found in caves, and so they created dragon lore."

"I think they may be out there," Hua said hopefully with a little shrug. "We can't just write off the existence of something because we've never seen it with our own eyes."

The witches lapsed into a thoughtful silence at this.

Sarah, however, felt fascinated by this mention of a warlock. Though Michael seemed like an ordinary attorney, he had been a warlock privately for many years, and Sarah had never really bothered to consider the reality of his magical practice since she had been such a skeptic as a young adult. Her own father could have been a powerful warlock, or so Lativia had told her, but he had denied his magical powers and chosen a nonmagical existence. "Can you tell me more about warlocks?" She finally broke the silence.

"Male energy works differently with magic," Margaret explained. "They sense things around them differently and put out energy differently. They often use their own spellbooks for that reason, a different type of magic."

"In that case, Earl couldn't use Lativia's spells?" Sarah asked.

"He could," Daisy said, "but he obtained his own copy of her spells, and we were never able to read it; the book was magically coded in such a way that only its owner could read its words. Earl came from a different style of magic, anyway. Loved saying things in Latin, just to show off, but my, did it sound good. Sometimes, he would mumble Latin in his sleep." She sighed wistfully. Sarah realized that Daisy had never stopped having feelings for Earl Reid, the warlock.

"Anyway," Daisy changed the subject rapidly, her face reddening in contrast to her purple glasses and purple-tinged dreadlocks, "he's long gone now."

"So he dated Frida? After you?" Sarah was trying to make sense of the deep rivalry that seemed to drive a wedge between Frida and Daisy.

"Frida stole him," Daisy declared. "Tempted him with her grand talk and staring into his eyes and reading his palms, all of that. He claimed she understood him better than I did. But you know, I couldn't force him to stay. And in the end, neither could she. When he heard a rumor about a dragon, off he went, and neither of us could keep him here."

"Warlocks aren't that loyal," Hua lamented. "That's why they seldom fit into covens. They just don't know how to stick together and work as a team the way women do. Lone wolves, you could say."

Daisy finally reached the front of the line and entered a polling booth. Then it was Sarah's turn. Sarah felt nervous as she stared at the three names listed on the paper ballot. *"Which one should I choose?"* she telepathically asked Addie, who was leaning against her legs. She finally checked Hua's name and threw her ballot into the shoebox with a slit cut in the top that served as a ballot box.

"Good choice, Sarah," Addie said, looking into Sarah's eyes.

"Psst," came a tiny voice. The shrillness was incredibly familiar.

Sarah set down her pen and looked around, trying to locate Clover Figcreek. She finally spotted the tiny faery perched on the corner of the ballot booth, her wings shimmery in the harsh fluorescent lights of the gym.

"There is about to be trouble," Clover Figcreek said ominously.

"What kind of trouble?" Sarah hissed, hoping no one could hear her talking to what would appear to be thin air.

"I don't like it," Clover Figcreek went on, starting to change from brown to blue.

Sarah cringed, hoping that Clover Figcreek was not about to start crying and wailing. "Does it have to do with the fox and the good luck charms? Or Oscar?"

"With everything!" Clover Figcreek wailed. "And you have to stop it!"

"Stop what? I can't stop anything if I don't know what to stop!" Sarah cried, exasperated. She realized that she had raised her voice a bit too much.

"Please! The town is divided! People can't agree! And with the town divided, well, you know what happened last time. Madras was able to move in and burn our beloved forest!" Clover Figcreek dramatically clapped her hands to her cheeks and began to tremble.

Sarah knew she couldn't take any more time in the booth without seeming suspicious and she already spoke too loud—enough to maybe raise a bit of suspicion. She promised Clover Figcreek she would see what she could do, and then she exited. Waving goodbye to Hua and Margaret, who were directly behind her, Sarah went to find Eli.

"That was weird," she told Addie as she searched for her boyfriend in the crowds. "What do you think she was talking about?"

"*Possibly that?*" Addie pointed her nose toward a group of people who had started arguing in front of the gymnasium's doors, pointing at each other and hurling vicious names.

Eli emerged from the crowd with Jenna, warning the people to calm down and disperse lest they wanted disturbing the peace charges.

"Rough morning, huh?" Sarah said, catching up to Eli and planting a kiss on his lips.

Eli appeared stressed. "Very," he agreed. "I've been investigating a vandalism case all morning."

"Roger's car was spray-painted with the word, 'Commie'!" Jenna rolled her eyes. "I can't believe this little election is spurring this much controversy."

"I worry things might get violent. We're going to have to stay here and keep an eye out," Eli said cautiously. "You be careful," he added, gazing down at Sarah fondly.

Sarah loved Eli's protective streak. It felt good to have a person care about her well-being. "Addie will stick up for me," she assured him with a laugh. Addie barked in agreement.

Eli was distracted as another fight broke out; he ran to break it up with Jenna. Sarah shook her head, wondering if Addie was right and the Leekins were simply concerned about the political division within Witchland. Never before had she seen people so divided—not even when they were campaigning against witches and accusing Daisy of murdering Peter Atticos, the town clerk, last fall. This really could bode ill for the town and the woods they all sought to protect.

Though she was worried, she decided there was nothing else to do but go home and relax with a law book. The results of the election would not be announced until that evening, anyway.

CHAPTER TEN

Susan Lake oversaw the dance and barbecue in the town square, where she would announce the results of the election.

The day had been clear and sunny, up until everyone started to assemble in the square around five. Then a menacing rumble from the dark clouds clustering above with rapid speed attracted more than a few worried looks skyward. The band and the smoker had already been set up in the open, and rain would be disastrous.

Just as Landon fired up the giant smoker and began to lay out burgers and ribs, the clouds decided to let down a torrent of icy rain. Angry orange flames shot into the air where the raindrops struck the hot grill. Landon jumped back, then cried out in pain as his hurt back seized up. It seemed that there would be no grilling, at least for the duration of the storm. He angrily slammed the heavy black lid of the smoker shut. Then he hobbled dejectedly back into the café where he worked.

Sarah and Eli took cover inside Javacadabra with several others, packing together like sardines. Other people ran into the other nearby businesses or their cars to avoid the downpour. Sarah watched as the folk rock band scrambled onstage to put away their instruments and electronics, which were dangerously exposed to the water pelting down from above. Positively soaked, the band members rushed into the café, carrying their fiddle and guitar cases and mopping their wet faces with their drenched sleeves.

"Towels! I brought towels!" Daisy cried, rushing in from the apothecary with an armload of towels that she had covered in a secret keep-dry spell. The musicians thanked her profusely as they attempted to dry off.

"That was weird. It didn't even look like rain until we were all gathered in the square," Sarah mused.

"Bad luck!" one of the musicians exclaimed.

Sarah glanced up at Eli. He pressed his lips into a thin line. "I wish we could've found those charms before today!" he lamented, quietly so no one could overhear him.

Suddenly, there was a loud crack of lightning, and a blinding light filled the café. Sarah turned to see another bolt of lightning strike a microphone still standing on the stage. Electricity shot down the microphone, along the cord, and then it erupted into a shower of violent white and blue sparks as soon as it reached the outlet box. With a boom and a flare of smoke, the box caught fire, and in a matter of seconds, the entire stage was burning. The flames raged, withering only slightly in the rain. Eli shouted and ran outside, soon joined by the volunteer firefighters of the town, who came running from all directions.

"Be careful!" Sarah shrieked after Eli. She hung behind, chewing her nails.

Within minutes, the firefighters and Eli had the fire out. At the same moment, the rain completely abated. There was an eerie moment of peace.

"That was . . . dramatic?" Daisy ventured. "I mean, really?"

But the town was now boiling over. Angry people swarmed into the square from every direction, shouting that they wanted to know who the new mayor of Witchland was. Susan Lake stood in front of the smoldering, blackened makeshift stage, shouting at the top of her lungs since she had no working microphone, "Everyone, please settle down! I am sorry to say that no one won the election—it was a tie between all three candidates. We're going to have to vote again."

Cries of rage and dismay rang through the crowd.

Sarah flinched and jumped back as the meaty thump of a well-landed punch resounded near her. She shrank back further as she realized the two men standing next to her had started fist fighting.

The entire square erupted into chaos. People began to berate and tackle each other. Elbows and fists flew through the air while furious voices rose in discordant pitches. One man picked up a chair and smashed it against someone else, who luckily appeared only dazed, not seriously hurt.

"Obviously we're not having a dance or a barbecue anymore!" Susan continued to yell, trying even harder to be heard over the commotion. "But we will still be having our baseball championship between the Magic Riders and Witchland Enchanted Bears within the next hour! Oh, c'mon, guys. Please stop it. This is not how we behave in Witchland!" Someone bumped into her violently, sending her reeling back. "Stop it!" she began to scream, turning red and completely losing her composure.

Alex ran up to Sarah, looking terrified. "Why is everyone fighting?" she asked, the edges of her mouth trembling. "All over a mere election?"

"I don't know, but this is bad," Sarah told her. "It's like . . . someone is stirring up trouble in this town."

"We have to figure out something!" Alex cried.

"We can't have this until the next ballot casting! I swear, ever since I lost that horseshoe . . ."

Sarah thought of Clover Figcreek turning blue and shrieking about trouble brewing. She gazed anxiously over the churning mess of yelling and punching people around her. Witchland was indeed in trouble—but what kind? Sarah had never seen the likes of this before in her life.

Suddenly, Eli's strong arms wrapped around her and began pulling her away from the crowd.

Eli's face was smeared with soot. His eyes blazed with stress and fury. "I'm going to break this up, but I wanted to make sure you're safe first."

Sarah nodded dumbly. "I now see why someone stole all of those charms. They want Witchland to be in turmoil! It worries me that maybe this individual is opening things up for Madras to step in. Or some other nefarious purpose. Their whole plan was to divide us completely, though, that much is clear."

"Yeah, well, they've succeeded then!" Eli agreed. He then ran back into the crowd, wielding his nightstick threateningly. "If you want to all spend the night in jail, keep it up!" he bellowed.

Mumbling among themselves people slowly began to break apart as they realized the futility of the brawling. They were normally a peaceful town, full of friends, so they realized this behavior was completely uncharacteristic. Neighbors stared at each other dumbly, amazed that they had come to blows for the first time in their lives. Friends mumbled sheepish apologies and shook hands. Brothers hugged begrudgingly, clearly not over their political differences but willing to stop fighting for the sake of their relationships. One woman had tugged another woman's wig off; now she helped her put it back on and adjust its lace cap. The folk musicians climbed onto the stage, shaking their heads and bemoaning the expensive electronic equipment they had lost to the lightning strike and electrical fire. The chemical smell from the blaze lingered harshly in the air. Sarah witnessed Hua and Margaret cautiously emerge from Daisy's apothecary, their faces reflecting the same shock that she herself felt. Unspoken questions hung in the now-still air—what was going on, who was going to be mayor, and what was the future of Witchland?

Susan Lake began to walk among the crowd, urging everyone to put this behind them and rekindle their sense of town spirit by going to the scheduled baseball game. At first, most people resisted, complaining they just wanted to go home, but gradually, with Daisy and a few others rallying behind Susan Lake, the town's spirits began to tentatively raise. The crowd began to move sluggishly toward the town's baseball diamond.

People kept muttering among themselves about how strange things had been for the past few days.

Sarah slowly followed, still stunned by all that had transpired. When she reached the diamond, she was amazed to see the field was not even muddy, despite the violent downpour that had occurred just moments earlier. The sky over the diamond was a perfect blue, and the sun shined on the ball players as they lined up outside their respective dugouts. It appeared as if it had rained everywhere *but* the diamond.

"What on earth is going on?" Sarah muttered to herself.

"And how can we fix it?" Addie added.

CHAPTER ELEVEN

THE BASEBALL GAME BEGAN WITH THE USUAL MASS singing of the American national anthem. The Enchanted Bears was the official Witchland team, composed mainly of volunteer firefighters, business owners, and parents who practiced in their spare time after work. The Magic Riders came from another small town nearby. Most of the baseball games were relaxed, friendly, and fun, but tonight, no one seemed to be smiling much. Sarah spotted Landon sitting glumly in the dugout of the Enchanted Bears. A smudge of soot on the tip of his nose added to his forlorn look.

Eli brought Sarah a vegan hot dog that he had made at home, since there was little chance of anything vegetable-based being served at the concession stand. Sarah smiled and pecked his cheek. "You're always thinking of me, and I love it," she said. She felt lucky to have such a thoughtful boyfriend. She had thought her marriage to Jeff was great up to its sudden and unexplained implosion—until she experienced love with Eli. Jeff had never thought of her that much or gone out of his way to do little things just to bring a smile to her face. *How did I get this lucky?* she thought, then shuddered and grew solemn at the word "lucky." Maybe luck was not something she should be thinking about right now, when it had clearly run out in Witchland.

"What are you thinking about? You look upset," Eli said.

"You know," Sarah said.

He nodded. "We'll get this mystery solved, trust me."

"I hope we can before we recast votes. This is not going to be pretty if it happens again! We need to do something, maybe alert people about Malorie. If we do that, we can postpone this whole thing until more information is gathered to help us all make a rational choice. I have to admit, it was hard even for me to vote."

Eli groaned. "Honestly? I wanted to vote for Malorie so badly, but what we discovered made it impossible for me."

"Tell me, did you vote for Hua?" Sarah asked.

He looked dejected. "I didn't vote at all."

"Eli!" Sarah gasped. "You could have been the one person to tip all of the votes in someone's favor!"

Eli looked guilty and didn't reply.

The game started with a terrible pitch by the visiting team. Just as it appeared the Enchanted Bears batter could not possibly hit the ball flying at him at a crazy angle, his bat made contact with it. The resounding smack made the Enchanted Bears fans burst into cheers. The ball flew directly into the mitt of the Magic Riders centerfielder, who fumbled and dropped it, surprised at his own stellar catch. He fell on his butt as he grabbed for it again, finally recovering it. The batter had almost reached second base when the centerfielder tossed the ball to the second baseman, who promptly dropped it as well.

No one knew whether or not to cheer. Tense silence hovered over the crowd as everyone crouched at the edge of their seats.

The second baseman reached between his legs and scooped up the ball. With a perfect toss, he threw it between the runner's legs and right into the third base-man's outstretched mitt, only to have him also drop it and comically chase it through the grass. Everyone gasped as the runner reached third base, out of breath, and then when his toe touched home base, they erupted in cries of joy.

"All right!" the grocer shouted. "That's my

Enchanted Bears!"

"The Magic Riders? More like Magic Losers!" some teenager booed, and Witchlanders laughed all around him.

The weird plays continued as the crowd watched, dumbfounded. The Enchanted Bears played as if they were pros against a Little League team. The Magic Riders didn't stand a chance. By halftime, the score was nineteen to zero.

"It's almost like there's *too much* luck now," Sarah muttered under her breath.

"What?" Eli inquired.

"Nothing. I'm just trying to figure this out," she replied. *Could the good luck charms be near here somewhere?*

"This is weird." He scratched his head, clearly as perplexed as everyone else.

Darkness descended over the diamond. The brown bats flying above chased mosquitoes underneath the floodlights. The Magic Riders team captain picked up a megaphone and mumbled an embarrassed call for a concessions break. Sweaty baseball players from both teams gathered in the middle of the field, trying to be good sports about their miserable loss as they swigged Gatorade.

It was a clear win in the end. The Enchanted Bears, in need of this victory, began to run around the field cheering with their arms in the air. Even Landon jumped up off the bench and began to run with them, no longer noticing his hurt back. The Magic Riders gathered in a huddle, watching them with perplexed looks and some bitterness. Never before had they played in such an uneven match.

"Magic Losers!" the teenagers began to jeer. The crowd erupted in jeers around them. Sarah stared, stunned that such ugliness could come from the normally sweet, friendly Witchlanders.

The team members began arguing. The Magic Riders umpire pushed the coach. He pushed back. Suddenly, all of them started brawling. The Enchanted Bears stopped running to watch, their mouths hanging open.

Once again, Witchland dissolved into ugly dissension as people ran down from the stands to join in the brawl.

The uproar roused Addie from her deep sleep. *"What's going on? Are they fighting again?"* she groaned.

Sarah rolled her eyes and stood up. "I'm going home, babe. Want to come with me?"

Eli glanced guiltily at the team members, who had begun to get in each other's faces and push each other. Someone was berating Landon for not knowing how to toss quarters. "Sure," he finally said. "Nothing I can do here. They'll be fine." He shouted for everyone to calm down but didn't bother to break the fights up a second time when they chose to ignore him.

The two dejectedly walked back to Sarah's place. Silence hung between them; neither of them knew what to say at this moment. Near her door, Kelvin was waiting for Addie. The two canines eagerly licked each other hello, and Sarah let Kelvin into the house to spend the night cuddling with Addie on her over-stuffed dog bed.

"I'm tired." Eli tugged off his heavy black boots and slumped onto Sarah's bed. He stretched out and added, "We need to get you a bigger bed." He often complained about Michael's old bed being too small.

Sarah took his feet onto her lap and began to massage them. "We have to find those good luck charms and get to the bottom of this. I have a hunch they're near that baseball diamond."

"What do your animal spirit guides say?" Eli suggested, trying to be helpful. Though he was hapless when it came to magic, it was cute to see how much he tried to be involved and informed.

Sarah shrugged unhappily. "The fox wants me to figure this out myself without using magical subterfuge, but I don't know how. I haven't heard from the lynx, and the wolf has nothing to say, either. The crows haven't been around much. I'm clueless, honestly."

"What about that reading Frida did on you the other day? There are other animals, right?" Eli prodded.

"Yes, but they haven't really been involved. Two of them haven't even revealed themselves to me yet. I don't even know what they are. I haven't seen them." Sarah sighed.

"Let's just get some rest," Eli finally said. "I can't think about this mess anymore!"

Sarah nodded in agreement. But after she showered and changed and snuggled into Eli's chest, which was gently rising and falling with his soft snores, she could not sleep. Her mind felt frazzled, almost like it was full of television static.

Suddenly, she heard something knock over in the kitchen. Addie got up from her bed, her tail wagging. "Michael, are you there?" Sarah called softly while lifting her head off of Eli's warm chest.

Michael entered the room in his wolf form, glowing blue. Sometimes he liked to visit in his wolf form to play with Addie and Kelvin. He tentatively approved of Kelvin, but Kelvin remained a bit standoffish toward Michael in return. Kelvin liked that Addie could transform into wolf form, but he wasn't that sure about the humans who possessed this talent.

"Michael, I need your help," Sarah moaned. "So much."

Michael slowly morphed back into his familiar human form. "Sarah," he said, sitting on the edge of the bed, "remember what I said about relying on a team to help you?"

"Yeah?" She propped herself up on an elbow to survey Michael, giving him her full attention.

"Witchland is divided right now. Teamwork and unity are what we all need," he went on. "This town has never done well with one person running things, or people arguing and divided. You have to unite people."

"That's the answer to all of this? It doesn't bring the good luck charms back," Sarah pointed out.

Michael shrugged. "Think of the witches who are divided, Frida and Daisy. They both have skills that could help you find the charms. If only they could work together to find where the charms might be, you three could recover them. That and you should use the help of Addie, with her sharp nose." He affectionately rubbed Addie's head, who was now standing at the base of the bed, her tail still wagging hard.

"Addie hasn't been able to sniff them out so far," Sarah said.

"Hey! I haven't been given anything to compare their scent with," Addie said petulantly.

"Sorry, girl, not trying to insult you! I am just saying that I have no idea where to start. You really think I could get Daisy and Frida to work together?

Their dislike seems to go way back." Sarah rubbed her forehead, trying to make sense of Michael's advice. It seemed sound, but was it actually feasible?

"At the heart of every rivalry is usually admiration and some form of affection," Michael told her. "Besides, they both love Witchland, and they love magic. They will surely be willing to put aside their differences for one task, anyway."

Sarah nodded thoughtfully. "Maybe Frida can divine where the charms are, and Addie can smell them, and then Daisy can use a spell to conjure them out of hiding." She smiled as the idea began to make more and more sense to her. "Thanks, Michael!"

"One tiny observation?" he added.

"What is that?"

"Did you notice that the rain did not fall on the baseball diamond, and the town's luck seemed concentrated there?" Michael shrugged. "Maybe something to look into."

"Your hunches always were right on," Sarah said, glowing with enthusiasm. "I already thought of that. I think the charms are there somewhere; we just have to hunt them out."

Just then, her phone began to ring. "Who is calling me at midnight?" she grumbled, rubbing her eyes as she retrieved her phone from her nightstand.

CHAPTER TWELVE

ELI GRUNTED, BUT DIDN'T WAKE, AT THE RINGING. Sarah moved into the other room and answered cautiously, since the number on the screen was unfamiliar but local. "Hello?" Sarah asked, concern in her voice.

"Sarah Spellwood?" a male voice asked.

"Who is this?"

"Oscar, Oscar Reedy," he said.

Sarah drew in her breath. "Oscar." With a final irritated glance at the red numbers on her digital clock, Sarah continued, "What can I help you with this late?"

"Oh, I'm sorry! The time got away from me after that bizarre election and then that even more bizarre baseball game tonight." He laughed with embarrassment. "Um, do you want to save this conversation for morning?"

"No, no, I'm eager to hear what you have to say." Sarah's heart began thudding. She didn't like hearing from him so late; it concerned her that something was seriously wrong.

"All right." Oscar cleared his throat. "Look, I'm an honest man with a reputation to protect. My business is actually fairly renowned on the East Coast. The idea of my reputation getting tainted by this—by this business with Dismas doesn't sit well with me. But I also care about these woods, and I know that without our delicate ecosystem, the hunting industry here will collapse, and we won't have anything left. To tell you the truth, I think you and I actually have a mutual interest in protecting the red fox."

"Sounds like we sure do." Sarah sat at her desk and clicked on the light.

Oscar cleared his throat again. "I actually appreciate your animal conservation work. Only a fool would fail to see the benefits of such things."

"Well, thanks." Sarah was relieved that Oscar was a good and ethical hunter.

"Maybe you could, you know, work some of that same magic this time around?" Oscar laughed.

Sarah froze. "Magic?" Did Oscar know more than he should? Not everyone in town knew of her magical powers, and she wanted to keep it that way, for her protection as well as the entire Wolf Coven's. Magic was not exactly a widely embraced practice. Witches had been persecuted for centuries, and they still were.

"Well, whatever it is you did before," he explained. "Lynx have been flourishing since you came here last year and got Dismas locked up! The state has given them protected status up here, too, which he was violating. It's illegal to shoot them. Now, it's not illegal to hunt foxes, but . . . I can see how it would be an issue now."

"I know you weren't in support of what he had been doing." Sarah grinned, relieved. "Yeah, I can try to work some of my magic." She winked at Addie, who was listening fervently. Michael had now gone, satisfied his work was done and he could rest for a while. "What's going on, though?"

"Here's the thing, my hands are tied, but yours aren't. There's been some complaints about a fox seen in town, maybe more than one fox. I thought I'd host one or two more guests before I can't anymore and I have to shut this place down for good. I had a gentleman, Lester, come in with a turkey tag yesterday. But tonight I caught him tracking the fox. I'm not convinced that's a good idea. They're not overpopulated, so killing them off could harm the ecosystem. Plus, this is a designated wildlife preserve on this side of the mountain, and he's trying to hunt where hunting is not permitted by law. I explicitly told him he can only hunt on the other side of Mount Katribus, but it seemed to go in one ear and out the other. I'm not a game warden, so there's not really anything I can do besides report him to the appropriate authorities, and they never did anything when I reported Dismas. I really need you to protect the fox."

"I can do that." Sarah nodded vigorously.

"And if you scare this man off, or get him arrested for hunting in town limits or something, I wouldn't necessarily be upset," Oscar added. "What he's doing isn't right. He doesn't care about or respect our forest at all, and any real hunter knows that you have to practice some environmental stewardship or else your whole livelihood dries up. We depend on the ecosystem, too, because when the balance is tipped off, we lose our game."

"Understood," Sarah said. She told Oscar goodbye and hung up. Then she looked at Addie. "You ready to work some magic, girl?"

She and Addie both began the transformation into wolves.

Sarah still was not used to the strange physical sensations of the transformation. Her skin itched as fur burst from each follicle; her eyes hurt as they became laser focused over her snout; her bones cracked as they changed shape and formed an entirely new canine skeleton; and her nails ached as they burst forth into cruelly curved claws. Finally, she experienced the drop to the ground and the change in gravity that meant she was officially on all fours. The rush of scents that assaulted her nose overwhelmed her; she instantly regretted the perfume she had spritzed on before going out earlier, which still hovered around her in a nauseating, alcoholic cloud.

"How can you stand my perfume?" she asked Addie, coughing slightly.

"You get used to the stench, I suppose," Addie said. Addie was also still transforming, her golden mixed-breed body growing leaner and stauncher, her muscles rippling under a new coat of thick silver fur. Her eyes hardened, and her nose became sharper, her ears more pointed and sensitive.

Sarah looked at Addie, her slightly smaller sister, and the two nodded at each other. It was time to work their magic!

Kelvin awoke, his light sleep easily disrupted by the sensations of their transformation. *"And what are we doing tonight?"* he asked, sounding rather amused.

He loved when he saw his girlfriend become a full-fledged wolf. Addie had once confided in Sarah that when she went into the woods to see Kelvin, she turned into a wolf and spent her time with him like that, only shedding her wolf persona to stay safe in the town limits. While Sarah worried about Addie in wolf form, since people were likely to shoot wolves due to a lack of education about the mythical threats they posed to humans, she was happy that Addie was getting in touch with her wild, authentic spirit. It would be any dog's dream to slip into wolf form and join the wild at any time, unimpeded by yards and gates and leashes.

"We're saving the fox," Addie informed Kelvin.

Kelvin scoffed. *"That little red weasel thing? I can't tell if it's a cat or a dog, but it's definitely a pipsqueak."*

"The fox is more important than you realize," Sarah chided him.

He turned his startling yellow eyes on Sarah. *"Right,"* he said, clearly unsettled by this human in wolf form.

"Tell me, do you want to help or not?" Sarah goaded him. The wolf's help would be an asset in the dangerous woods as well as against this formidable hunter who flagrantly disobeyed rules.

"Sure, why not?" he said flippantly. But Sarah could tell that underneath his cool exterior, he was thrilled by the promise of action, too.

Camouflaging with the trees and stones around them, the three loped through town, unseen by anyone who might still be up. Sarah noticed lights still on in the baseball field and voices. Clearly the town was not sleeping well, but she would get to that tomorrow with the supernatural team Michael had advised her to assemble. Tonight called for a different type of action!

When they reached the deep woods near the lodge, skirting fox traps that the hunter had laid out, they spotted the hunter himself standing there. He was using a new technology: heat signature goggles. As he searched the woods for traces of animal life, his lips parted in a sinister sneer. Sarah frowned. The fox had little hope against the sheer amount of technology and armor that Lester had acquired.

"You keep an eye on him and try not to let him see your heat signature. I'm not sure if the invisibility spell works for heat," Sarah told Kelvin and Addie. *"I'm going to search for the fox."*

She began to dash through the woods, branches smoothly gliding across her coat. She loved the power that rippled through her muscles as she traversed the dark grounds, sailing over rocks and branches as if a sixth sense told her they were there. The scents of squirrels, hedgehogs, and rabbits filled her nostrils; the earth smelled especially good as her paws turned up clumps of moss and rotting leaves, exposing the forest floor.

Her sensitive ears recognized human feet tramping behind her. Big, heavy boots with thick soles. She froze, realizing that Lester was probably the only one prowling the woods at this hour. He was on her trail!

Using her magic, she blended in with the tree she was near as Lester came into her line of sight. He snarled in frustration, putting down his goggles. "These animals! How do they keep getting away?" he growled.

He continued to move along, more interested in the fox than a wolf anyway. He most likely knew better than to slip up and kill a wolf with the number of people watching his every move.

Suddenly, Sarah smelled the fox. Its scent was unmistakable, sharp and clear as a bell, cutting through the air to her nose. She cautiously turned her head and spotted the little red-and-white animal crouched under a bush not ten feet away from her.

"Run!" she told it. *"You're in danger!"*

The fox only snickered. *"Maybe you are, but I'm just fine!"* Then, with a twitch of its tail, it darted out of the bush, directly into Lester's line of sight.

Lester grinned and began to level his rifle at it. "Got you, you little bugger," he muttered.

But the fox danced off into the trees, its laughter floating behind it like a taunt.

Lester grunted in rage. "These foxes are just pests!" He slung his rifle back over his shoulder and took off after the fox.

With his attention diverted, Sarah began to chase him, determined to keep him from harming her potential next spirit guide. He didn't even notice her paws crunching twigs and leaves, his attention was so laser focused on the little, evasive fox.

The three reached a small clearing. Lester stopped running and crouched down to observe the surroundings. He gingerly stepped over a log, his eyes riveted through his goggles on the fox, who stood tauntingly at the opposite end of the clearing. The fox held very still, twitching its tail, relishing every moment. Lester carefully slung down his rifle once again, leveled his sights on the fox, and began to engage the trigger.

"*Go!*" Sarah screamed at the fox.

The fox leaped up into the bushes and out of sight.

Furious, Lester pulled the trigger anyway. A bullet whizzed into the bushes with a deafening report. Several nesting birds and a bushy-tailed squirrel screamed in terror and escaped the bushes, their nocturnal home forsaken.

"*You killer!*" Sarah cried. In her wolf form, the potshot was especially upsetting. It sent every nerve in her body into a frenzy of instinctual terror and rage. She sensed the danger of this man in camouflage, and she hated his scent. As a wolf, the danger he posed was all the more real than when she was a human; she felt it in a primal way.

With a snarl, she flew through the air, knocking his rifle onto the ground. Lester yelped in shock as he lost his balance under Sarah's weight and fell to the ground. He turned to see what had attacked him, and his eyes widened. "The wolf I was following!" he cried. "What the—you're not supposed to attack me!" He covered his face with his arm, bellowing in terror about rabies.

"*You wish I had rabies!*" Sarah spat, leaping off of him. At that moment, she took on her human form.

Lester recoiled as he watched her become human. "What—what in the world . . ." He blanched and began to tremble violently. "I must be losing my mind! I must have taken too much Zoloft. I . . ."

With a horrified yell, he swatted for his rifle. Sarah realized the mortal danger she was in if she didn't restrain him somehow.

Just then, many Leekins began to pour from the trees and drop pine cones on his body. A whirring sound filled the air, and suddenly Blackberry Hoppers began to launch themselves from the brush, pelting his body with their tiny, hard bodies. They made insect sounds that filled the clearing with a deafening cacophony.

Kelvin and Addie also dashed into the clearing. Addie promptly locked her jaw around Lester's shooting arm without actually biting down, while Kelvin retrieved the rifle and dragged it far away.

"Would you stop hitting me with pine cones?" Kelvin barked at the Leekins.

"What the hell are you doing to me?" Lester roared. "Get off me, you wolves! And whoever is throwing pine cones at me, stop it, now!"

"Not until you leave these woods for good," Sarah declared.

Clover Figcreek landed on Sarah's shoulder, clinging to her coat with her toes, her wings still beating in case she needed to fly away rapidly. "I will happily restrain you with magical ropes if you require," she said to Lester, "but I hope that you will cooperate with us and do as we say."

Lester fixed his eyes on the tiny faery and gasped. Then, pale and shaking, he used his free hand to frantically search for a Bowie knife in his belt. His intent was clearly violent as he locked his fingers around it and then unsheathed it, aiming for Addie's throat. But then he fumbled with the knife as Sarah moved toward him. He was so disoriented she was able to knock his knife out of his hands, which caused him to accidentally slash the side of his pants open, baring his hairy, pale leg. Embarrassed, he dropped the knife and glanced at Sarah.

Sarah's bold action had worked. Lester seemed to be cowering from her as if she was still a wild wolf. In that second, Sarah grinned, knowing that she had won.

"I believe Oscar Reedy told you that you can't hunt here and you are not to go after anything but turkeys," Sarah declared. "Please tell me then, why are you out here again, going after a fox?"

"I—it's just a fox!" he whimpered.

"No, the fox is a critical part of the ecosystem here. But whether you care about the fox itself or not, there are laws all hunters must abide by. And you are breaking so many of them right now!" Sarah snarled. "What if there are kids playing around in these woods, couples taking midnight strolls? You are blindly shooting into brush. You could seriously hurt or kill somebody! I should call Officer Eli and get you arrested."

"No! I really don't want to lose my hunting license! My family counts on me for venison and turkey throughout the year." Lester struggled to get away from her, then froze with a whimper when Addie bore down on his arm slightly harder with her fangs. He grimaced, then stopped moving. "Ow! You're going to break my arm!"

"Then I suggest you get out of *our* woods, now!" Clover Figcreek declared. Sarah was stunned at the sheer might of her voice as it echoed through the trees.

"What *are* you?" Lester blinked at the Leekin, just when another Blackberry Hopper collided into his face. He smacked at it, and it crumpled to the ground.

Then he recoiled in horror when he saw it was not an ordinary grasshopper.

Lily Silverhopper and some other Hoppers shrieked in despair and rushed toward their fallen comrade. As Lily attempted to revive the crumpled Hopper, Lester tried to scramble away, but then he fainted.

Sarah gave him her green-eyed stare while she waited for his eyelids to flutter back open. "Pack your bags, get in your vehicle, and leave! Tonight!" she ordered.

Lester nodded pitifully. His jaw had begun to tremble, like a kid who had been caught shoplifting and was begging the shopkeeper not to call his mom. "I didn't break any laws!" he muttered. "Please don't go calling the game warden on me!"

"No, I won't call the game warden yet, but you broke our laws in this forest. You forget, there's more to life than just following the state laws. Humans may be apex predators, but you're still dependent on nature. Today, we are proving that to you, and we are ensuring that you regret messing with nature. We have our own way of doing things here in Witchland. And you're not welcome here anymore."

"And please don't kill me," he pleaded.

"I'm not violent like that, and I don't believe in

killing living things. You just need to get your things and leave," Sarah replied.

"Forever!" Clover Figcreek screamed.

Lester scrambled up and ran off into the trees, leaving behind his rifle in Kelvin's maw.

Sarah paused for a second to see if the fallen Blackberry Hopper would survive. The others had pulled her up and were supporting her between their long bodies. Lily Silverhopper was using her hands to fashion a small carrier out of pine needles. "Will she be okay?" Sarah inquired.

"Yes, yes, she just has a broken leg. We have magic potions to heal her quickly," Lily Silverhopper replied. "You go make sure that man is gone for good."

"I will," Sarah promised. "Thanks for your help." She then took off after Lester, Addie bounding along at her side.

Kelvin had been hiding at the edge of the clearing with the gun, waiting for a sign of what to do with it. When he saw Lester was leaving, he dutifully joined Sarah and Addie and the Leekins chasing after Lester as he streaked through the trees. Lester kept glancing back at them fearfully, holding his hands up in the air in submission. The three then waited outside of the lodge as Lester disappeared inside and then emerged, laden with heavy packs and weapons, and loaded them into a Jeep parked in front.

"Sorry it didn't work out!" Oscar stepped into the doorway and called after Lester. "I don't normally refund stays, but I'll go ahead and put the charge for the remaining five nights back on your card."

"Good! I definitely won't be coming back!" Lester cried. Then he noticed the wolves and Sarah at the edge of the parking lot. "I'm going," he said indignantly, trying to quell the shake and the high pitch in his voice.

Sarah folded her arms across her chest. "For how long?"

"Forever." He glanced at the trees towering blackly over them and then spat. "I'm never coming back to this creepy, forsaken forest again!"

"We'll always be watching for you," Sarah assured him.

Lester shot her one last look, betraying his deep fear of her, before hopping into the driver's seat and slamming the door. He rapidly backed up and then sped away, leaving the scent of burning rubber lingering behind him.

"Do you think we finally got rid of him?" Sarah asked Addie.

"*Yep!*" Addie agreed. Then she looked up at Sarah, her eyes full of adoration. "*You are the top dog!*"

"Thank you!" Oscar called with a wave. Sarah waved back.

Oscar began to descend the wooden steps in front of his lodge. Sarah realized he was sweating and shaking. "Are you okay?" she asked him.

"That sure was some performance out there, Sarah. I saw it all on a game cam I have installed out there. Wondered what the hell wolves were doing, boldly attacking a human like that, because you and I both know wolves don't normally attack humans, ever. But there were three wolves just scaring the heck out of Lester, and then one of them morphed into—you."

Sarah gulped. "I guess you know my secret now." She laughed nervously, gauging Oscar carefully for his reaction.

Oscar shook his head. "You Spellwoods. I guess the rumors are true. What was that, some kind of spell that changes you into a wolf?"

"Shapeshifting, actually. It's an ability, not a spell. My dog can also shapeshift. Some animals are capable of it," Sarah explained. To prove Sarah's point, Addie began to morph into her normal golden mixed-collie form.

Oscar simply stared for a moment before shaking his head. "I suppose my suspicions were true about you, about these woods, about this town. I come from Dallas, see, and I once swore I saw a man turn into a swan on Possum Kingdom Lake. Strangest thing ever. My dad said I had been out in the heat too long, to come back in the boat and take a nap. My whole life I knew about things, just didn't want to admit it." He gazed past Sarah's shoulder, and she realized he was looking at Clover Figcreek. "I knew about the Leekins, sure, and I didn't mind them that much. But witchcraft and shapeshifting? Now I'll never be the same."

"I hope not," Clover Figcreek squeaked. "We want you to stop hunting."

Sarah sighed. "Clover Figcreek, hunting is an important and ethical trade if done right. It balances populations of animals and provides nourishment, sometimes for families who can't afford meat from the grocery store. What Oscar does is actually a good thing."

Clover Figcreek merely shuddered and cried, "Aieeeeee! He's still a Hunter, the King of Hunters!"

Oscar looked sad. "I think it's past my bedtime," he said finally.

"Good night, Oscar," Sarah called.

Oscar nodded slowly as he went inside. The door clicked as he locked it, and Sarah realized he felt a bit of fear toward her, mixed in with his respect. She had never wanted to scare anyone with her powers—save for Lester, of course—and she hoped Oscar would come to regard her warmly again.

Sarah turned at the sound of chipper laughter behind her. There was the fox, boldly standing in the parking lot of the hunting lodge, not even trying to hide from the two wolves and the human before it.

"*Nice job,*" it said.

Sarah slowly began to grin. "You really think that's the case?"

The fox snickered again. "*Don't get too cocky, now. You still haven't solved the mystery of the good luck charms. That will prove how clever you really are.*"

"I think I have," Sarah replied. "I think they're near the baseball diamond." Suddenly, with a smirk, Sarah added, "It's a strange coincidence that these thefts started around the election. I thought it might be one of the candidates, but now I am beginning to wonder. Could this be a test from you? Did you take them and hide them somewhere, possibly the baseball diamond?"

"*Why would I ever do something like that?*" the fox taunted, the mock innocence in its voice irking Sarah.

"Because you want to cause trouble and test my mettle," Sarah responded, her voice faltering. She really was not quite sure if the fox had actually committed the thefts, but she knew that the fox was getting its desired result. "Besides, you are able to hide and slink around far more easily than any human could."

The fox laughed and quivered its tail. "*One thing is for sure, you solve this, find all of the charms, and figure out my purpose, then you gain me as a spirit animal guide. Remember that."*

"Want me to catch it for you?" Kelvin offered. *"I can outrun that thing in two seconds."* Then he added under his breath, *"And kill it in one. Not that you'd let me, but you know, I'm just saying."*

Sarah groaned and shook her head. The fox took off, pleased with itself. "I don't even know if I want that sarcastic little creature as a spirit guide," she muttered. "It has been nothing but trouble."

"It sure is rude," Addie agreed. *"And really, is it a dog or a cat?"*

"Neither." Sarah sighed. "It's a fox, through and through."

The three trekked back to town, another night's work protecting Witchland and the forest done. On the hike down the mountain, the Leekins swarmed around them, yipping in joy and celebrating the departure of the despised Hunter. Lily Silverhopper also joined the party to announce that her comrade would be just fine and now had her leg in a splint and was drinking healing tea.

Sarah collapsed into bed, thoroughly exhausted. Eli smiled and moaned slightly in his sleep as he rolled over and clasped his strong arms around her. He had no idea that she had been gone.

But in the morning, he did notice the leaves and

moss bits stuck to her hair, and he picked them out while she dozed before he got up to make coffee. He didn't say a word about it. All he knew was that Witchland may have its problems, but ultimately, it was safe for another day because of his girlfriend and her dog. "It's not so bad dating a witch," he murmured to Addie, affectionately scratching behind her ears.

CHAPTER THIRTEEN

Following Michael Howler's hunch, Sarah walked to the baseball diamond in the morning, Addie trotting by her side. "I'm going to test the energy around the baseball diamond to see if I can get some answers," she told Addie. Straddling the lower bench on the bleachers, she reached for the cards she slipped into her back pocket before she left her house. "I'm not completely sure why I think these cards will help get us some answers, but I saw them on the counter and figured they may have some good luck power."

Addie wagged her tail. "*Whatever works, but I will tell you, Sarah, all I can smell are the hot dogs from last night's game.*"

Sarah rolled her eyes. "You and that disgusting processed fake meat you like! You're lucky I make your food and don't feed you stuff like that."

"*I wouldn't mind it,*" Addie admitted.

Sarah sighed. Then she shuffled a deck of cards and randomly drew one. An ace of diamonds. She drew another: an ace of spades. With mounting incredulity, she drew the last two aces from the deck. With a cry of triumph, she flung the cards down. "The luck is undoubtedly concentrated here. I just know the charms are here!"

"*Like I told you. I can't smell a thing. Just beer. And sweat. And hot dogs,*" Addie told her.

"We're going hunting," she told Addie. Maybe that was another interpretation to the hunter card Frida had drawn during her reading.

She walked around the diamond, looking for disturbed dirt. Of course, there were many patches of disturbed dirt and broken turf from the game and the skirmish last night. She investigated each spot just in case, finding nothing. Addie couldn't detect any unusual scents—though of course she didn't know what she was supposed to be sniffing for anyway, having no scent to compare it to.

Sarah peeled up the plates and dug with her hands. Then Addie took over digging for her. Still nothing.

In the woods along the edge of the diamond, she peered between brush and tree trunks, hoping to catch sight of something unusual. There was nothing out of the ordinary, no disturbed ground or strange mounds as if something might have been buried. "What on earth," she muttered under her breath.

"*I found something!*" Addie crowed proudly.

Sarah jogged up to her. Addie was pointing her nose excitedly at a piece of red fur, with a perfect tip of white. Sarah picked it up and turned it over in the sun. She frowned. "Even more evidence incriminating that fox."

"*She peed everywhere, too,*" Addie informed her.

"She? The fox is a female?" Sarah felt strangely affected by this information, as she realized the fox was even more of an enigma than she had previously thought. Honestly, she knew nothing about this creature, yet she was supposed to trust her and gain her as a guide? However, Sarah also liked that the fox was female because gaining her as an animal guide made all of her guides female. She was part of a coven of sisters, with an all-female guide team—how cool was that?

"*Yup. She's a she,*" Addie said.

After a long while of searching, Sarah felt defeated. "That's it, then. Michael was right. I can't do this on my own." She rubbed her lower back, which ached from stooping over and searching.

"*Okeydokey, what are we going to do?*" Addie inquired.

"We're going to find Frida and Daisy," Sarah said, her voice full of determination and grit as she thought of the daunting task of uniting two rival witches. From her experience with Madras and Lativia dueling on the mountain, she knew that witches made formidable enemies.

"*Oh, boy,*" Addie groaned. "*A sister fight is coming. Or should I say, witch fight?*"

"They better not fight." Sarah sighed. "Too much is at stake here. We need to save Witchland before it destroys itself." Flashbacks to the violence and discord of the night before made her more determined than ever to put a stop to this mischief. At this point, Sarah wasn't even thinking about gaining the fox as her spirit animal guide; she only wanted to bring peace and order back to her beloved town, and maybe work out who the next mayor should be. Poor Susan Lake needed a break; she couldn't act as stand-in mayor forever.

Frida was in her parlor, steeping a cup of deliciously fragrant tea, when Sarah knocked. "Come in," she trilled.

Sarah gingerly entered the overdecorated fortune parlor. The smell of incense was overpowering, and the scent of the tea was intoxicating. Sarah felt a bit woozy.

"What is that?" she asked, gesturing toward the chipped mug in Frida's hand.

"Oh, just a little something Margaret gave me," she replied. "It turns your mouth purple, but gives you more pep than coffee! And without the jitters."

Sarah smiled. "I love Margaret and Hua's teas." She sat across from Frida, surveying her face intently.

Frida suddenly looked awkward. "Oh, my stars. I sense you are about to ask me to do something hard, something to do with . . . Daisy?"

Disconcerted by Frida's eerie sense of perception, Sarah cleared her throat. "I am just requesting that you two set aside your differences and help me find the good luck charms. I think you may have an idea why, given what happened yesterday."

"Ah, yes, that fiasco. Honestly, I do understand." Frida sighed. "I'm all for it. Your friend Daisy is the one with the problem."

"I think you both have problems with each other," Sarah reminded her. "And pointing fingers at who has the problem doesn't solve anything for anyone."

"She's just so . . ." Frida made a face.

Sarah didn't even want to hear it. She put her hand up and said, "Michael Howler suggested it. And I know not to shut out my mentor's advice anymore out of pride. That's a very crucial lesson I've learned the past few days." She smiled to herself, sure that Michael was listening on the other side of the veil that divided the living and the dead, gloating that he had made his point.

Frida's face softened. "I loved Michael." She sighed as she lifted the tea bag from her cup and laid it gently on the saucer. "What does Michael want us to do?"

"I know the charms are by the baseball diamond," Sarah explained. "That much is obvious, given the weird game last night and the fact I drew all aces from a deck of cards and other ridiculous things that beat all the odds earlier. But I hunted everywhere and couldn't find them. Addie can't sniff them out. And here is the thing—I need you to divine where they may be."

"Oh, dear." Frida looked worried. "We psychics tend to operate poorly under that kind of pressure. Ask us to predict the lottery or find your lost keys and we're fairly useless. But count on us to hear a message from beyond about your dead aunt's secret love child while we're in the supermarket!"

"That's where Daisy can help you. She can use a summoning spell or something to bring the charms up from their hiding place. She's a very powerful witch." Sarah noticed the slight glimmer of jealousy in Frida's eyes before it quickly passed.

"I'm willing to try if Daisy is," Frida finally acquiesced. Then she started to smile. "You know, I actually liked Daisy, back in school anyway. She's always been the cheekiest thing. Her voodoo background is absolutely breathtaking—voodoo is quite powerful stuff, since they have the power of many gods behind them. We used to have contests to see who could move books or chairs telekinetically, or who could speak to ghosts the most clearly." She settled back in her chair, a wistful look on her face. "Crystal Ernestine MacBeth forbid competitions in her house, but we did it anyway!"

"You are telling me Earl Reid was the only thing that came between you two?" Sarah asked incredulously.

"I suppose our competitive nature got a bit out of hand when he entered the picture. You know, I always had a thing for him, from the moment I first laid eyes on him." Her eyes sparkled. "He had charisma. But come to find out, all warlocks do! Something about the magic and the Latin, ooh la la."

Sarah found herself thinking of Eli. Something about that uniform hugging his muscles! "I guess he was your type, huh?" She laughed. "Cops are my type."

"Daisy got to him first. I was hurt! He was her type, too. And it just got out of hand from there. When he came to me, well, I suppose I might have flaunted it a bit. . . ." Frida looked sheepish.

"It sounds like he's been gone quite a while, and I hope you two can settle something," Sarah prompted, standing. "Do you want to come with me to the apothecary?"

"Just one thing . . ." Frida began slowly. "I still talk to him."

"Oh?" Sarah could sense the roiling cloud of drama that could arise from this, and she had no desire to see any more conflict and division. "Probably best if we don't mention it to Daisy, right?"

"But should we really turn this new leaf with a lie?" Frida wrung her hands.

Sarah groaned. "Maybe after we find the charms we can talk about it?" she suggested testily, not sure Daisy ever needed to find this out. Did Daisy also still hear from this charismatic warlock everyone seemed to be head over heels in love with?

Frida agreed good-naturedly and followed Sarah to the apothecary. She hesitated at the door, pretending to admire its ornate woodwork, but Sarah could tell she was nervous about entering her long-time nemesis's business. Perhaps Daisy had even placed some sort of hex around the place to repel Frida.

"Come on," she gently urged Frida.

The two women entered the shop. Daisy looked up from her potion—which, from the looks of it, was not going well. A scorched smell filled the air of the little apothecary, along with an oily smoke.

"Someone burned something!" Frida trilled, propping the door open.

Daisy looked annoyed. "Thanks for pointing out the obvious! What brings you here, Frida? Need some wart-be-gone?"

Frida simmered.

"All right," Sarah cut to the chase. "I need you two to set aside your differences for a minute! There's something much more important at hand, and I want both of you to help me." Then she laid out the details to Daisy, whose eyes widened behind her purple-framed glasses.

"Well," Daisy quickly agreed, "since losing my lucky potion vial, I've been experiencing the worst sales of my life, and burning potions every day." She glanced at Frida. "I'm in. If you are."

"I am." Frida sniffed.

The three witches made their way to the baseball diamond, Addie trailing along behind them. *"They seem to be getting along,"* Addie commented to Sarah, who nodded, relieved.

At the field, Frida paused, holding her arms out. A smile began to spread across her bright red lips. "Ah, yes, I can feel them here!" Suddenly, as if she were a bloodhound on the trail of a scent, she began walking rapidly in zigzags around the diamond. Finally, she paused right above the pitching mound.

"I looked there but couldn't find anything," Sarah muttered.

Addie looked up at her sympathetically.

Daisy approached the mound. "Don't tell me—they're here?"

Frida nodded. "Buried very, very deep."

Daisy held her hands over the mound to sense the depth. She took a deep breath of exasperation as she realized it was much deeper than she had anticipated. "It's not impossible," she said, gesticulating for Frida to step off the mound. Then she began to chant a spell, and the dirt began to swirl up in a mini-tornado. The flurry of earth spilled onto the turf next to the mound as a huge pit began to form.

Here and now.
We bring forth the elemental force of Air.
I call to the season's breeze and the howling wind,
To move the earth and show us the invisible.
I call you here,
To infuse my intention with your twirling gifts
And reveal those items hidden.
Air, I call to thee.

Soon, the smoothly curved form of the canoe bottom appeared. A silver brooch gleamed next to it. Daisy wrinkled her forehead in concentration. Sarah joined her, lending her strength to the tremendous effort needed to free the good luck charms from the dirt's hold and levitate them up into the air. They then gently laid the items on the turf with magic, as well.

All of the missing items lay in the sun. Daisy muttered a cleaning spell to get rid of the residual dirt. Then she scooped up her lucky potion vial, clutching it to her chest with gratitude.

Sarah picked up the horseshoe for Alex and the brooch for Landon. With some disgust, she also scooped up Harriet's enameled newt eye. "We'll need to call Chris to come pick this up," Sarah commented about the canoe.

"What about this mess?" Frida indicated the dirt piled on the turf. "The city guys won't be too happy about the baseball diamond being destroyed."

Daisy and Sarah joined forces again to return the dirt to the pit.

Frida clapped, looking thrilled. "Oh, I miss watching you practice magic!" she cried. "You know, I spend most of my time among the magically disinclined; therefore, it's refreshing to see this!"

Daisy begrudgingly said, "I miss your clairvoyance. Nothing can hide from you for too long!"

"You said you might not even be able to sense where the charms were." Sarah grinned proudly, hugging Frida. "Thank you. There are some people who are really going to be grateful to get these items back."

"They had such a strong energy, I couldn't miss them," Frida agreed. "By the way, speaking of vibes . . ." She wheeled to face Daisy. "I sense Earl on you. All over you, in fact."

Daisy looked startled, then defensive. "I just received a letter from him, yes. Why? Why do you care?"

Frida surveyed her, then asked crisply, "Does he tell you that he pines over you every night and sees your reflection in the cave pools, too?"

"Yes, he says that to you, too?" Daisy looked incensed when Frida nodded, and then both witches' faces crumpled into sudden laughter.

"What a loser!" Daisy howled.

"He hasn't come up with any new lines over the last ten years, has he?" Frida slapped her thighs.

Sarah found herself laughing, too, when something red flashed in her peripheral vision. Without a second thought, she sprinted after the fox, her human form rapidly changing into a wolf's as she weaved around trees. She heard Frida whistle behind her, impressed by her complete change into a sleek, strong wolf with thick silver fur. Addie started to chase after her, but she shouted, *"Addie, wait!"* Like a good dog, Addie sat and waited, though she was still straining to see and hear what transpired without her in the woods.

Once Sarah and the fox were out of earshot from the others, the fox suddenly stopped running. Sarah nearly tripped, but her superior senses as a wolf helped her avoid the blunder. She froze in the center of the clearing, inhaling the fox's rich, musky scent, memorizing her face and coat.

"What are you in such a hurry for?" the fox asked with her characteristic snideness.

"Why are you such a troublemaker? What did you take the good luck charms for? You know you ruined Chris's crop this year," Sarah replied angrily. *"And Daisy lost a lot of money at her shop. Landon actually hurt his back! And Harriet can't even see! You really hurt people, and I'm supposed to consider you a spirit guide?"*

The fox threw her head back to laugh heartily.

Sarah growled in frustration. *"I don't think this is very funny!"*

"All right, all right. You figured me out fair and square. I only wanted to show you how Witchland looks when it's divided, and how it must be united to operate properly," the fox replied.

The fox then showed her teeth in what appeared to

be a grin, but then Sarah realized something strange was happening. Her sharp, little teeth were growing smaller and more square. Her ears were receding. Her red hair began to shrink away from her skin, remaining only on top of her head, as her back legs lengthened and her front legs shortened into her trunk. Soon, she had taken on a fully human form.

Sarah gasped. It was Malorie! She was wearing blue coveralls and a mischievous grin. "It's me! Ta-da!"

"You're a witch?" Sarah inquired.

I'm a fox who can shapeshift into a human," Malorie replied.

"You mean a human who can shapeshift into a fox," Sarah corrected.

"No," Malorie said impatiently. "I was born a fox. I *am* a fox. Just like Addie, some animals are shapeshifters. I just happen to be able to shapeshift into human form."

Sarah gasped. "I—I didn't even know that was a thing."

"Oh, it's a thing." Malorie grinned triumphantly. "All that spying you did on me, and you couldn't figure it out! No one has been able to for a long time."

"I knew something was off about you. Michael said he couldn't place it, but you were different, and Addie couldn't place your scent. I looked into your background and couldn't find anything. I worried you were some sort of plant by Madras," Sarah said.

"Oh, never." Malorie laughed heartily. "I hate Madras with a passion. And all of the hunting and development and greed she represents. I was sickened when plans to develop the woods started a few years ago. My solution was to turn into a human permanently, dig up a treasure that was buried in the woods to pay for my businesses with cash, and start fresh in a way that wouldn't put me in harm's way."

"That's amazing," Sarah said. "I had no clue you were the fox at all! You always seem to be in two places at once. How were you in the woods, then also in your bed and breakfast the other day?"

She grinned. "I'm just really, really fast. You saw me evade Lester last night."

Sarah nodded. "You are impressively fast. Were you also the one who stole Frida's cards and laid them out for me?"

"Exactly. I had to lead you to Frida, and then have you unite Frida and Daisy. You all will make a powerful force!"

"Keep in mind everything you do has an ultimate purpose." Sarah shook her head. "You always think a few steps ahead of everyone else. I suppose that's why you have done so well at business?"

"I do like to tamper with good luck. How do you

think I've made such a killing in this town's hospitality industry, when it previously had no tourists?" Malorie flexed her bicep to show a four-leaf clover tattoo, glaring in its bright greenness. "I practically made the tourism industry and hospitality industry here! I grew it from a place where only a few Lativia-obsessed spooks came a few times a year to a place where families come to hike and enjoy nature. That boosted the economy and the luck of the town overall. Everything I do, I do for the good of others. Such is the fox way; we are called devious, deceptive, tricksters, liars, and more, but we just have our own ways of making things happen."

"I can see that, and I really do appreciate all that you've done for the town. But you've also done a lot of bad, even if you don't see it. I want some of your cunning, but not the trickery. Do you now consider yourself my animal spirit guide?" Inquired Sarah.

Malorie shrugged. "I'm not personally your guide, no. I'm only one manifestation of the fox, but I will grant you the inherent wisdom and coyness of the fox. It is now a part of you. If you are ever in trouble and a fox is nearby, then you can call upon it for help and it will gladly aid you. Having these powers makes you a more complete witch."

Sarah frowned, then argued, "But nothing you have done has been particularly good. I already knew

Witchland needed to be united; it was obvious, and I didn't need you to hurt people like Chris and Landon to prove that to me. And I expressly asked you about the good luck charms, and you lied to my face! How can I possibly trust you?" Sarah put her hands squarely on her hips. "It seems to me like the fox is not a very good spirit guide, to be frank with you."

Malorie surveyed Sarah coolly before nodding approvingly. "Your heart is in the right place, I can see. Reminds me of Lativia." She grinned. "But you fail to see the bigger picture, which is typical of humans. You see, I set everything right with Chris Graylock. I gave his crops a little extra dusting of good luck. Now they'll grow extra fast and make up for time lost. And Daisy? She'll find an influx of tourists will help her business grow tenfold in the next few months. We small business owners help each other out. As for Landon, that back injury was about to happen anyway, and it will heal soon enough. Now he's determined to lose weight and take better care of himself. Alex is about to enjoy a bit of good luck with a new romance, someone who actually deserves her." Malorie winked. "And Harriet might just be willing to see an ophthalmologist finally because she's realized her newt eye is not the most effective tool for combating blindness. See, in every bad thing that happens, there is some good. That is the fox way, guiding people to destiny, sometimes with bad and sometimes with good."

Sarah was appeased, though this whole thing still seemed very strange to her. She felt glad to see the fox in its real form and also for the chance to get to know the real Malorie. "That's certainly an important power. I'm glad I have it now. Clarify one thing for me. Are you still running for mayor? Or did you just do that to cause trouble and bring about destiny in your fox way?"

"What do you think my purpose was, proving how united Witchland needs to be?" Malorie challenged Sarah. "Think about it and get back to me. There is something specific I am aiming for, and I want your help achieving it."

Sarah thought hard. "Um . . . that everyone should vote for you?" she asked testily, still uncertain of Malorie's true nature. After all, the fox had not been exactly forthcoming with her.

Malorie rolled her eyes. "Do you really believe I'm that petty? That's disappointing. You forget I am a fox, just like you are a wolf! The trivial, egotistical concerns of humans are beneath me."

Sarah got a sudden bright idea. "You're running for mayor and doing all of this because you believe Witchland can benefit from everyone working together, as a part of your plan, but maybe also Roger's and Hua's."

"Bingo!" Malorie's eyes flashed as she grinned and waved her hand toward the town. "People are notoriously one-track-minded. We need to show them how three mayors can make the difference this town needs. How everyone can ultimately be mayor in their own way."

"I think that's a fantastic idea," Sarah admitted, her heart swelling with excitement. "I mean, I really like it."

"Yeah? Then help me convince these people of it. Right now, they're not exactly open to something that, shall I say, modern?" Malorie shrugged.

"Well," Sarah admitted reticently, "what you're talking about is democracy, which is technically pretty old."

"You know what I mean," Malorie said pointedly. "How often is a democracy actually democratic? Not often! People still treat everything like an oligarchy, even this town's government. And we need to change that. Witchland deserves better. It deserves money, and well-mended streets, and a library roof that doesn't leak."

"And more forest to protect." Sarah grinned. "I'm all in. Let's do this."

Malorie grinned and nodded. Then she began to transform back into a fox. Once she was on all fours and completely covered in red fur save for the white tip of her tail, she gave Sarah a challenging look before taking off toward town again. Sarah laughed and transformed back into a wolf herself to give chase. The two ran through the trees and brush, laughing and nipping at each other, now good friends.

CHAPTER FOURTEEN

CHRIS ARRIVED AT THE BASEBALL DIAMOND IN HIS battered farm truck. He scratched his head in puzzlement at his family's canoe, lying on the pristine baseball diamond, while Daisy and Frida stood by it. "Strange things happen in this town," was all he commented when Sarah told him a fox had stolen the charm to create mischief. He had lived in Witchland all his life, as had many generations of his family; not much surprised him anymore.

Sarah laughed. "Indeed, they do." She helped him heave the heavy canoe into his truck bed. "I hope it's not scratched," she added, admiring the beautifully sculpted and highly polished wood. The animals painted on it were stunning in their vivid color.

"Nothing I can't buff out," Chris replied. Then he

nodded at her. "Thank you." His voice was deeply laden with gratitude.

Sarah smiled. "Don't mention it. How are your crops doing, by the way?"

"Oddest thing. They had a growth spurt last night. The powdery mildew is all gone!"

Sarah nodded. "I think all of our luck is about to turn around. By the way, come by the town hall tonight and bring your kids. We have to talk about the new mayor."

Chris shook his head, clearly not relishing the idea. "I don't want my kids to be around a bunch of fighting and people acting stupid."

Sarah shook her head. "I just decided that I'm hosting a town meeting, and I want everyone to be there. It will definitely be peaceful."

Chris promised he would be there and drove off. Just as he left, Landon and Alex came up to the diamond together, engrossed in conversation.

"I didn't know you two knew each other." Sarah smiled as she handed each of them their respective charms.

"We just met," Alex said, grinning with dazzling brightness. She clutched the horseshoe to her chest. "Oh, how I missed you!" she crooned to it.

Landon's eyes sparkled with moisture as he accepted his grandmother's brooch from Sarah. "Well,

I never thought I'd see this again. And my back already feels better." He also pressed it to his chest, clearly cherishing the final piece of his grandmother that he had left.

"A fox took them," Sarah explained.

Alex stared at her, mouth agape. "A fox? How did you find them all?"

"Some digging." Sarah shrugged. She heard Daisy titter in laughter behind her.

Alex narrowed her eyes. She, too, was beginning to see how strange things happened in Witchland. "Okay." She turned to Landon with a twinkle in her narrowed eyes. "So, you were saying about how you make a mean pot of chili?"

"The best you've ever tasted," Landon boasted.

"Let's see what you got," Alex replied, grinning flirtatiously.

Sarah thought back to Malorie's promise that Alex was about to find a great guy and felt her heart bursting with happiness. She loved this town and how things worked out, bringing people together. She was determined to keep it that way. With the fox's powers added to her own, she now might be able to execute similar beautiful things with similar cunning. "When you two are finished with dinner, be sure to come by the town hall," she told them. "I have a great idea to sort out this whole mess with the mayor situation."

"Sounds good," they both agreed before ambling off, still deep in conversation.

"That's that, then," Daisy said, dusting off her hands. She looked a bit frazzled, and frizzy bits of hair emerged from her dreads. She was exhausted after the magical energy expenditure she had just engaged in.

Sarah realized she felt pretty winded, too—she still had to get used to the tired feeling that arose whenever she performed any sort of telekinetic spell—but, of course, there was still work to do. *It never stops here in Witchland, but I wouldn't have it any other way,* Sarah thought with a smile.

"How about we go to Margaret and Hua's and have a nice cup of energizing tea?" Frida proposed.

"The purple stuff?" Sarah inquired.

"Exactly. It's made for times like these. And you can fill us in on whatever happened back there with that fox." Frida winked and linked her arms through Sarah's and Daisy's, marching them in the direction of Margaret and Hua's.

While they drank tea, Sarah gave an abridged version of the events that had transpired of late, including her encounter with Lester and her conversation with Malorie. When she concluded, all four witches stared at her, awed.

"I thought there was something about Malorie," Michael commented from behind Sarah. Frida and

Sarah both glanced at him, able to hear him. No one else knew he had entered the room, but Hua and Margaret could tell by how Sarah glanced behind her that he had joined the little meeting of the coven. They both called, "Hi, old neighbor!"

"Oh, Michael, hi." Daisy beamed. "I always love hearing from you. You have no idea how deeply you are missed here."

Sarah could sense that Michael was happy to know he had not been forgotten. Life moved on without him, but everyone still very much loved and missed him.

"Anyway"—Sarah wiped her lips, observing the bright purple stain on the napkin and hoping she could get the color out of her mouth before speaking to the town—"I really need to speak to the whole town and tell them of Malorie's plan. It's a great plan, really."

"I'm certainly open to the idea, but I must admit, Malorie doesn't seem like much of a team player," Hua mused. "I worry she is doing this for her own personal gain somehow."

"Remember, she is part fox," Margaret said. "Her entire motivation is getting us to work together."

"Yes, and plenty of evil people are shapeshifters, too. Look at Madras," Hua argued.

Sarah shuddered, recalling Madras's demonic wolf form. "Madras didn't look like a real wolf, though," she said. "Malorie is a fox who becomes a person. She isn't corrupted by anything evil, I don't think. She just likes to play games, as foxes do."

"And, Frida?" Margaret asked. "What do you gather from all of this?"

Frida shut her eyes and fell silent in concentration. "I sense peace and prosperity ahead," she said slowly. "United we stand."

Hence the witches all eventually agreed to Malorie's plan to elect three mayors. Sarah began to prepare herself for the meeting, which included chewing on spearmint leaves from the greenhouse to remove the purple stains from her mouth. The tea was worse at staining tongues than a gas station slushy! At least it worked as Frida said it would; Sarah instantly felt elated and driven, ready to take on the world.

Sarah approached the town hall, pleased but also nervous to see a large crowd already spilling out of its huge front doors. *News travels quickly here,* she thought. Apparently, telling just a few people and posting a sign at the grocery store was enough to assemble everyone. Susan Lake ushered her into the hall, where almost all of Witchland sat or stood, staring at her intently.

Sarah stepped up to the microphone Susan had set

up for her and cleared her throat. "Hello, everyone," she began.

Silence fell over the crowd. Their intent faces made Sarah nervous.

"I think we can all agree that election night was a fiasco and we need to do it over again. Right?" Sarah plowed on.

People reticently began to nod in agreement. They exchanged uneasy looks, undoubtedly trying to gauge if more anger and violence might be brewing.

"Can I get Hua, Roger, and Malorie to please join me up here?" Sarah requested.

The three candidates stood up from the front row and assembled on either side of Sarah. Malorie winked at Sarah. Sarah wondered how she had missed the fact Malorie was a fox. It was strikingly obvious now, from her hair to her sharp nose to the mischievous twinkle of intellect in her eyes.

"We're very divided right now. And we've seen how that hurts us as a community and brings down our morale," Sarah continued. "Maybe instead of being divided, we should focus on being more united. That is what has gotten us through the many trials and tribulations that this town has faced over the years. We have to continue sticking together, or the town will fall apart again. Each of these three candidates represents a great idea, a lot of ambition, and several of Witchland's best interests. But none of them are perfect on their own, which is why we are not in agreement on who is ideal for our town. Malorie has great business insight that she can use to fix the town's budget problem; Hua has great knowledge of the biology, botany, and history of the area to bring it front and center for tourism to flourish even more; and Roger has the brilliant idea of expanding our state forestland. All three of them can help each other make Witchland better than ever, without changing it from the town that we all cherish. Here is my suggestion: Let's consider appointing all three as mayor and having them work together to bring about the changes they all want—that *we* all want."

Sarah paused, waiting for a reaction. The crowd was silent for a second before several people raised their voices at once.

"Yeah, that's nice and all, but how can you have three mayors?"

"They won't agree on anything and won't get anything done!"

Hua held up her hands. "All right, everyone. I propose that we abolish the idea of mayors altogether and instead use a council. We three will sit on the council as elected representatives, but everyone is allowed a vote on important issues at weekly meetings at the town hall."

Malorie added, "I second that!"

"I do, too," Roger said.

The crowd was silent for a minute. Then they began to agree, as they realized the merits of the idea.

"Wait," Susan Lake spoke up. "You're proposing to restructure the entire municipal government of Witchland? That will take months, if not years, to accomplish! There is paperwork to fill out, bylaws to file . . ."

"We will figure it out as we go along," Malorie assured her. "Witchland is not exactly a bureaucratic place. I'm sure people are open to some flexibility."

Susan looked uneasy. "But with no precedent, I can see this becoming a complete disaster."

"I can see us working together and supporting each other so that it doesn't become a disaster," Roger spoke up. "We may not see eye to eye on everything, but we all share one thing in common: our love for this town and its forestland. And we're not going to let anything get between us."

"Especially not silly politics!" Hua said.

"Here, here," someone called out from the crowd.

"If we're all in agreement on this, then maybe we should cast a vote? All in favor, say 'aye,'" Sarah called out.

"What about ballots?" Susan gasped.

"Aye!" Almost everyone raised their hands. Alex counted the votes, jotting them down.

"All not in favor, say 'nay,'" Sarah prompted.

Other than Susan, no one spoke. Chris raised his hand, but he simply wanted to know if people might be able to cast votes even if they missed the weekly meetings at the town hall. He then agreed when the three candidates confirmed that was possible. Some other people had other logistical questions, which they soon worked out. Susan even relented in time, agreeing to help them draft a new town constitution and work out the kinks of their new structure.

"Shall we bring on the festivities?" the grocer bellowed when all of the voting was finished. "We need a do-over from last time!"

Everyone raised their voices in enthusiastic agreement. They then began to move outside into the square, preparing for the impromptu celebration. Food seemed to magically appear on a long table, potluck style, and one of the townsfolk started walking around on stilts. Someone else was playing the accordion.

Landon brought out the smoker and began to make his famous burgers and ribs, filling the town square with smoke that made Addie's mouth water. Addie looked up at Sarah with pleading eyes, and Sarah nodded permissively. Addie cried, *"All right!"* and ran up to the smoker, sitting down right beside Landon, begging for a drop of grease or anything even vaguely edible to fall her way. Landon smiled at her and tossed her a chunk of sausage, which she eagerly caught midair, her jaw snapping shut with delight.

People gathered in the center of the town square, talking, hugging, and exchanging ideas for how to improve Witchland at the first town hall meeting. The folk band set up, this time without their amps and microphones, and began to play. A few couples danced. Landon left someone else in charge of the grilling to take a few turns on the cobblestone square with Alex, whose cheeks were flushed with happiness.

Someone brought out a giant beach ball. It looked extremely out of place in the setting of New Hampshire forest and the misty Mount Katribus in the background, but everyone laughed as they began to bat the beach ball overhead around the square.

Across the square, Sarah spotted Harriet, with Edgar perched on her shoulder. She hurried over to her and placed the enameled newt eye in her hand. The witch in the pointy hat grinned as she closed her fist around the eye, feeling what it was. "My luck and my sight are back," she said, placing the eye in her front pocket.

"Maybe we could take you to a doctor? What if you lose that thing again?" Sarah prompted.

Harriet narrowed her eyes, but then nodded slowly. "Maybe. They'll laugh me out of the room with my getup though!"

"So let them. You're not afraid of being different," Sarah said gently.

"But I can't even drive," she continued to argue. "The nearest eye doctor is in Smithvale."

"I'll happily give you a ride," Sarah offered.

"In that rattletrap?" Harriet jokingly referred to Sarah's Beamer, which was far from a rattletrap.

"Yes, unless you'd prefer to fly on a broom," Sarah replied. She was beginning to feel more at ease around Harriet and more able to tease back.

Harriet broke into a toothy grin, then she reticently agreed. "Two witches off to the big city in a luxury vehicle, oh boy!" She began singing a strange song as she walked away.

After Harriet left, Sarah stood to the side, observing the townsfolk enjoying themselves, when she noticed Oscar Reedy sauntering up to Malorie. Malorie was standing with a group of small business owners discussing ideas to bring new business into the town. As Oscar greeted her, Sarah could see Malorie seethe with tension. The other people speaking to her moved away, but Sarah moved closer in case there was trouble.

"I'm very excited to begin working with you, Miss Vulpes," Oscar said.

"I am as well," she responded coolly.

"Perhaps we can set this competition between us

aside and work together for the greater good of the town? Perhaps we can help stall the acquisition of the woods behind Mount Katribus in order to keep it legal to hunt in?" Oscar prodded.

"You'll have to speak to the others; I'm not the only mayor," she responded, voice now cold.

Oscar looked taken aback. "May I ask why you seem vehemently opposed to my ideas? I've been a staunch supporter of yours since the minute you declared you were running."

"Maybe it's because you have my brother's head mounted in your hunting lodge? You took his life and made him a piece of art," she snapped.

Oscar stared, dumbfounded. "What on earth are you talking about, your brother's head?" "That fox mounted right above your staircase," Malorie replied.

Then realization began to dance across his face. "Are you one of those shapeshifters, too?" Oscar gasped.

"I am a fox in human form, yes. I know you are already aware that there is more to this place than meets the eye," Malorie went on. "And there is more to me than meets the eye. I trust you can keep a secret."

"Of course." Oscar took a step back and noticed Sarah hanging out in the vicinity. He shot her a nervous smile and said, "Oh, hello, Sarah!"

Sarah was happy that he greeted her, after his

fearful reaction to her shapeshifting. She moved to stand next to Malorie and said, "I feel terrible for your loss, Malorie."

"It was one of those defining moments that convinced me to become a human nearly full-time," she replied. Then she bored into Oscar with her eyes. "Death is one thing, and hunting is one thing; displaying my brother like his life meant nothing more than becoming a conversation piece for your business is entirely another."

"I will take that fox down immediately." Oscar gulped. "I—I really had no idea."

"Perhaps we could do a memorial for your brother? A proper funeral?" Sarah suggested.

"I think that's what he deserves," Malorie agreed, still glaring at Oscar.

"We'll do a funeral, of course. How can I ever apologize enough to you? Honestly, I didn't know." Oscar stumbled over his words, looking horrified.

"You can't," Malorie replied. "But for the sake of this town and my livelihood, I will work with you civilly."

Oscar nodded slowly. "I really didn't think of animals having, you know, consciousness."

"No one does," Malorie said simply. "It takes an enlightened human to know animals have emotions."

Oscar bowed his head to Malorie and then Sarah.

Then he walked away, seeming shocked and confused. Malorie thanked Sarah for her idea about the funeral, and then someone stole away her attention for more business talk.

Eli then approached Sarah. "May I have this dance?" he asked, holding out his hand and bowing like a Victorian gentleman.

"Is the handsomest guy here really asking me to dance?" Sarah pretended to be shocked.

"Only if the prettiest lady here will have me," Eli replied.

Sarah and Eli danced to a few songs and enjoyed sharing a huge bowl of meatless chili that Landon made specially for Sarah. "Thank you," Landon mouthed to her as he gave her the large bowl.

"What was that about?" Eli inquired, noticing the immense gratitude with which Landon had spoken to her.

"Oh! I have a lot to catch you up on." Sarah gasped, realizing how he knew nothing of the entire night before and the day in the baseball diamond. "But maybe not right here. Want to go home?"

"I'm ready." He nodded, casting one last glance over the town square. It was already dark, but the people showed no sign of being tired. "I don't think I'm really needed here," he added.

"I think they're fine." Sarah smiled. She led him by

the hand back to her house and began to regale him with the tale of how she had solved the mystery of the missing luck charms.

"I just love you." Eli laughed. "I'm the cop here, but you always solve every mystery, a step ahead of me!"

"We just make a good team," Sarah responded.

CHAPTER FIFTEEN

A LIGHT DRIZZLE FELL OVER THE FOREST THE NEXT morning, dusting the tree leaves in silver mist. It was relatively cool as Sarah pulled on her rain jacket and went for a hike up the mountain with Addie and Kelvin.

A brown blur flew into her line of sight and slowed, eventually becoming visible as Clover Figcreek in flight. "Whee!" she squeaked.

"We did it," Sarah agreed.

"Lativia wants to talk to you," Clover Figcreek informed her.

"I had a feeling she would want to. That's why I came for the hike. That, and to enjoy the woods in the rain." Sarah looked around at the beautiful trees drinking their fill and the lush green moss and dripping ferns tickling down their trunks. The forest always took her breath away.

"Follow me!" Clover Figcreek urged. She began to whizz up the path, and the brown blurs of other Leekins in flight soon joined her, filling the air with a sound similar to hummingbirds. In the brush, Sarah could hear the distinct clacking sounds of Blackberry Hoppers hopping along as well.

Kelvin groaned. *"I hate these faery things."*

"Hate is a really strong word," Sarah admonished him.

"They're annoying." He groaned again. *"They hurt my ears."*

"They're part of why you're still here," Addie reminded him. *"They take care of the forest and its creatures, including you."*

He groaned a final time but didn't say anything more. The scent of a squirrel suddenly caught his attention. He and Addie took off together into the ferns, never straying too far from Sarah, though.

Sarah reached the ghostly clearing at the top of the mountain. Ghosts wandered through the perpetual gloom of the deeply shaded clearing, holding their goblets of blue wine high, their laughter and chatter ringing off the trees eerily. Sarah's arm hairs stood on end with the intense sensation of static electricity that always accompanied this place. The Leekins slowly descended from flight and formed a pyramid. Lativia gradually materialized near them on her throne, holding her own goblet of wine.

"Hi, Lativia," Sarah said respectfully.

"Hello." Lativia appraised Sarah in her lime green rain jacket. "Such strange clothes you all wear in these times. That blouse is rather like what I imagined those little creatures from the heavens would wear."

"You mean you had aliens in your time?" Sarah was baffled by this reference.

Lativia seemed perturbed by the question. "We can't be alone, can we? The Puritans often saw lights in the sky and little men descending from them."

Sarah stared. She had certainly not expected a conversation about UFOs and aliens with her ancestor from the seventeenth century! Witchland's surprises never ended. *Don't tell me I'm going to have to deal with an alien invasion of this town at some point,* she thought sarcastically.

"Anyway, how does it feel to have *four* animal spirit guides?" Lativia went on, as if the conversation opening had not been at all odd.

"I am proud," Sarah admitted. "I really like having these powers and these animals who trust in me. It's an immense honor."

"It took me much longer to acquire the fox as one of my spirit animals. The fact her spirit chose you so early in your magical development tells me that she has many wonderful things in store for you," Lativia complimented Sarah.

"Was the fox difficult for you, too? Lying, deceiving, and masquerading as a human?" Sarah asked.

Lativia sighed. "Let's say that the fox and I were not necessarily friends at first." Then she smiled wanly. "You have done fabulously, and I'm proud of you. You are indeed my blood. And you have saved Witchland yet again, this time from itself. It is an important lesson—we can destroy the things we love best if we are not careful."

Sarah nodded, absorbing the magnitude of the lesson. "I'm just glad that all is better now."

Lativia nodded. "As am I. But I'm afraid I cannot rest just yet. And neither can you. We still have work to do—things ahead of us."

"Trouble?" Sarah asked.

"Troubles never completely go away; please never become complacent." Lativia then began to fade into the air, and Sarah turned away from the clearing, perplexed.

"She always does that," she complained to Addie. "What kind of trouble is ahead?"

"*Looks like we still have work to do,*" Addie said, enthusiasm in her voice.

"Will I ever be able to sleep at night, not worrying

about the next thing?" Sarah sighed. Then she brightened up, realizing that her usefulness would never end in this town. Furthermore, she would always have a challenge awaiting her, something to keep her busy. *I guess there's nothing wrong with still having work to do,* she thought with renewed enthusiasm and cheer.

A SMALL GROUP ASSEMBLED AT OSCAR REEDY'S hunting lodge for what was meant to be a late memorial service for Malorie's brother. There were Susie and Karen with their white cat Zeva; Margaret and Hua, who had grown and arranged the flowers for the service; Sarah and Eli with Addie and Kelvin lying at their feet, Kelvin cloaked by an invisibility spell to protect him; Officer Jenna Mora and her new boyfriend, the handsome Officer Peter Jett; Daisy and Frida, who stood next to each other, giving no indication of their previous rivalry; Harriet with Edgar perched on her shoulder, wearing thick new glasses after Sarah took her to the eye doctor last week; and, finally, Oscar and Malorie. Most people in the town had no clue about Malorie's true identity—no one did, in fact, but the people gathered at the memorial service.

Oscar brought out the stuffed mount of Malorie's brother. "Oh, Timber," Malorie moaned in grief when she saw the handsome, full-grown fox head in Oscar's hands.

Oscar looked guilty as he gently placed the head beside a small grave. At the head of the grave was a headstone, declaring Timber Vulpes's date of death, and several flower arrangements set up by Margaret and Hua. Sarah had ordered the headstone with Malorie earlier that week. When the funeral director wanted to know the date of birth, Sarah looked at Malorie, and Malorie shrugged unknowingly. "Sometime during spring?" she guessed. Looking puzzled, the director had left the date of birth off.

"Malorie, would you like to say some words?" Oscar cleared his throat.

Malorie stepped up to the grave and cleared her throat. "I wish you could have accompanied me on this journey, Timber, but I know that you are watching me from above, proud. I will continue to fight for your justice and the justice of our kind. You may think I'm a traitor, living as a human, but it's what I had to do. I love you, dear brother." Tears spilled down her freckled cheeks as she stepped back.

Everyone else in the group murmured goodbye and

thanked Timber for his life. Oscar then began to bury the head. Sarah wondered what he might be thinking, if his distraught expression had anything to do with the money he was losing by burying such a display.

Oscar soon answered her question. After everyone had laid flowers on Timber's grave, Oscar cleared his throat and said, "I just wanted to let everyone here know that I have decided to officially close the Witchland Hunting Lodge and Guide Service. Not only is my business no longer possible now that the town is moving to acquire the land behind Mount Katribus, but I no longer have the heart to separate families in this fashion. I have decided to turn my lodge into a nature preserve, where people can stay before enjoying our massive forest in an ethical and ecologically conscious manner."

Everyone began to grin and clap. "That's a wonderful idea," Susie and Karen praised. "We'll provide discounted treats and eats at Javacadabra to your guests!"

"Thank you." Oscar smiled. "Further, I hope you all understand this, but I will not be shutting down my new hunting lodge in Maine. I am a businessman, and a hunter at heart. It's how I grew up, eating deer, moose, bear. I can't completely disown my lifeblood and give up the one thing I'm good at, which is guiding." He gave a humble smile. "Therefore, I have decided to dedicate that lodge to education about ethical hunting and hosting only ethical hunters during deer and elk seasons. The heads of animals will no longer adorn my walls. I do not mean to rip apart animal families and show it off; I simply wish to perpetuate the circle of life."

Again, everyone nodded in approval. Even Malorie seemed pleased. "I'm glad something good came of this," she said, "and I support you keeping two small businesses open. We have to earn a livelihood. After all, I am a businesswoman at heart, even though I was born a fox."

As the service drew to a close, everyone went inside Oscar's for a lavish lunch and some of Oscar's home-brewed beer. Sarah looked over the faces gathered around the table and thought, *I'm lucky to have these people as friends. And no matter what lies ahead, I know these people have the best interests of Witchland at heart.*

CHAPTER SEVENTEEN

Eli came to Sarah's that night with a large loaf of French bread and two to-go bowls of something that was deliciously fragrant. "French onion soup with melted cashew cheese!" he crowed when she opened the door.

Sarah smiled as she let him in. "Wow, dinner! This is a nice surprise."

"There was a little French bistro near the place where the district law enforcement conference was held in Manchester," he said, smiling. As he set up dinner on the small kitchen table, he regaled her with stories about new self-defense techniques and a new type of radar that he had seen at the conference. Sarah set out silverware, lit a candle for the center of the table, and uncorked a bottle of her favorite Cabernet.

"That's all pretty fascinating," Sarah said. "Anything about using magic to aid law enforcement?" She grinned cheekily.

Eli laughed. "Nope, that's just the Witchland police department's little secret." He leaned over and pecked her cheek as she sat next to him. "By the way, what do you think of Jenna's new boyfriend?"

"He seems really great for her." Sarah grinned. She had always felt a bit bad that Jenna had formerly had feelings for Eli. While Jenna had gracefully conceded him to Sarah, Sarah always wondered if she might have residual feelings for him. The fact she had a new boyfriend was good news indeed.

"Yep. He seems nice." He tore off a hunk of bread to dip in his soup.

"That's wonderful! Everybody seems to be meeting someone special now. It's a good spring indeed." Sarah beamed, relishing the love and romance blossoming all around her, and also within her own heart.

"I bet you think he's hot," Eli teased. "Seeing as you have a thing for men in uniform."

Sarah shook her head. "Honestly, I don't even notice anyone else anymore. You are the only one I think about."

Eli paused his eating. "You know, that actually really means a lot. I suppose I've told you a bit about my history." He then coughed. Bringing up his ex-wife and her affair with his law enforcement partner in Buffalo always made him uncomfortable.

Sarah placed a reassuring hand on his arm, admiring the firmness of his bicep underneath. "Of course. I've been meaning to ask, do you ever hear from her?"

"Not a word. My understanding is she married Paul and then they split up eight months later." He shrugged. "I used to laugh and say she deserved it. But now I honestly just wish her the best."

"I can understand that. I felt pretty bitter when Jeff moved to Chicago and got a new job at a fancy law firm. I even kind of hoped he would get fired or something, just for my own vindication. But now I just hope he's doing what he needs to do, and I even hope he met someone." She sighed. "I suppose time heals all wounds."

"And those wounds brought us together," Eli commented.

Sarah surveyed him, enjoying every inch of his face, his hair, his strong body. Then she smiled. "You know, I'm really grateful for you. You just accept me as I am."

"Who wouldn't?" Eli scoffed. "You're amazing."

Sarah shrugged. "Most men wouldn't be too into magical spells and talking dogs and forest faeries. You remember how my parents were so nervous about me being a crow." She and Eli giggled at the memory.

"You know, I really don't know that much about your family. Since you've met mine, I think I should meet yours," Sarah suggested.

"I don't speak to my father much since he left when I was little. Sometimes he'll send a birthday card or a Christmas card. My mom is a lawyer in Buffalo, and she's often too busy to speak to me, too. She certainly thought I was crazy for moving here! Last I talked to her, she was going on an Alaskan cruise." Eli grinned. "I think she has a boyfriend, but she doesn't like to admit it. She has to be an independent woman, all of the time."

"Does she know about me?" Sarah's eyes sparkled with teasing.

Eli nodded.

"What did you tell her?" Now Sarah was genuinely curious. She tried to picture Eli's mom, and all she could envision was an imposing, intimidating matriarch who never smiled.

"I told her that you're an environmental activist and lawyer, and she asked if you're a hippie." Eli laughed. "I showed her a picture, and she said she never saw me with a redhead. And when I mentioned you're a Spellwood, to tell you the truth, she didn't say anything at all."

"Oh." Sarah pulled back, disappointed. "That doesn't sound promising. Maybe I can meet her and convince her I'm good enough for her son."

Eli squeezed her hand. "You are good enough for me, no matter what my mom thinks. But of course, you will meet her. I want you to meet all of my family."

They then began planning a trip to meet his family.

When Eli excused himself to go home for a shower and some much-needed sleep, Sarah kissed him. She watched him walk away, feeling grateful. Addie told her, "*I love Eli!*"

Sarah was just about to tuck herself into bed when someone rapped lightly on her door. She opened it to see Frida standing there with another animal oracle card in her hand.

"Oh, hi," Sarah said warmly, welcoming Frida inside.

"Oh, I don't want to come in and intrude. I'm terribly sorry to show up this late. I didn't mean to be rude, but I had a calling to do another reading on you, and I . . . I drew the fifth card." Frida beamed as she held the card out, facedown.

Sarah took it and turned it over.

It was a black bear sitting on his haunches with his nose pointed toward the sky.

"Is this my next animal?" Sarah gasped.

"Yes." Frida beamed. "Now reflect on what the bear means to you and keep your eyes peeled for him to appear in the near future!"

Curious about how a forgotten murder can change Sarah and Addie's life forever?

Get Pawtrayal Now!

http://getbook.at/pawtrayal

A NOTE FROM MELANIE

*Ms. Addie Pants and I love foxes. In fact, one comes
to visit our compost pile every night. We see it on
our webcam. She looks like a fox . . . Don't you
think?*

Thanks so much for reading this book. I love the growing sisterhood and friendship of Sarah's Wolf Coven. Don't you?

This story was special to me as I studied foxes in graduate school. I got to observe a wild fox momma and her babies. The love and care this fox momma showed was so nurturing. Such highly intelligent creatures.

But lynx, wolves, crows, and foxes are not the only spirit animals for Sarah to discover. Check out the next book and I can't wait for you to hear about their next journey.

Stay tuned for a sneak preview of the fifth book in the series, *Pawtrayal*, which is now available on Amazon. Click here to skip the preview and read the whole magical book. http://getbook.at/pawtrayal

Did you enjoy *Impawsible Mischief?*
Get the next book in the series
http://getbook.at/pawtrayal

Pawtrayal
The Spellwood Witches, Book 5

While she's basking in love's glow, an old enemy strikes. Can a clever witch solve a mystical mystery before the wicked win?

Sarah Spellwood has found the most adorable house and can't wait to share it with her gorgeous boyfriend. Except it's haunted by the ghostly victim of Witchland's only unsolved murder, so move-in day can't come until she cracks the thirty-year-old cold case. But no sooner does the supernatural sleuth pry open the past than her best witchy pal is snatched without a trace.

Certain her devious nemesis is behind the disappearance; Sarah and her chatty hound uncover clues that link both crimes. But with her bitter ex-husband in town and under the villain's spell, she'll need help from her new bear friends to avoid becoming ensnared by evil.

Can Sarah break the sinister enchantments and make sure everyone has a happily ever after?

Pawtrayal is the delightful fifth tale in *The Spellwood Witches* paranormal cozy mystery series. If you like wise familiars, heartthrob romances, and captivating whodunits, then you'll love Melanie Snow's mystical brainteaser.

Buy Pawtrayal to come to the magical rescue today! http://getbook.at/pawtrayal

ENJOY AN EXCERPT FROM
PAWTRAYAL

Do you want to find out if Sarah can help an agitated ghost rest in peace? Can a witch break the sinister enchantments and make sure everyone has a happily ever after? *You will be able to find out in the next book of the series: Pawtrayal!*

Pawtrayal is now available on Amazon. Download your copy right now! http://getbook.at/pawtrayal

You're not ready to get your own copy? Enjoy part of the first chapter for free on the next page!

Pawtrayal

Chapter 1

The bear sat on his haunches. Through the leafy trees, he could see Sarah Spellwood moving about her warmly lit kitchen and stirring something in a pot. The aroma of food wafted toward him, making him salivate. He figured he might just have to rifle through her trash bin later in hopes of finding some leftovers. But then he hung his head, knowing he couldn't. Mournful memories of his distant cousin, trapped and taken to a town far from Witchland for the same offense, filled his mind. Humans discarded food to rot in their bins and then fiercely protected their trash; it made no sense, but the bear had realized long ago that he could never fully comprehend humans.

Sarah Spellwood was safe for another day, her magic free to grow stronger and for this the bear was content. But he still had to watch over her, for while she was fierce in her lynx, wolf, crow, and fox spirit magic, she was a relatively young witch, and a prime target of the dark forces because of her powerful Spellwood ancestry. She was also primarily stuck inside a fragile human body. There were so many dangers lurking, and others out to get her. She needed someone, something, to watch over her.

Then the bear observed the man, Sarah's mate, standing up to press his face into hers the way humans liked to do. He liked that man; he sensed that he would always protect Sarah and make her happy. She always seemed to smile more when he was near.

Sarah ladled the vegan spaghetti sauce over a plate of noodles. For the past year, in addition to studying magic, she had also been brushing up on her cooking skills, which had been sadly lacking. This dish actually seemed to turn out well, to her pleasant surprise.

Eli Strongheart observed her cooking uneasily from the kitchen table, where Addie, Sarah's trusty golden-collie mix, lay snoozing at his feet. The last time Sarah had cooked, she nearly cut off her finger because she wasn't paying attention. "That smells good," he finally commented, standing up to kiss her. He glanced at the pot of spaghetti, assessing the beautiful creation the love of his life conjured up.

Sarah beamed up at him. "I perfected this sauce the other day. I've been practicing. I am finding that I love the craft of cooking. It makes me feel very witchy. Now let's eat." She dished up the spaghetti, and Addie moved to stand next to her, begging.

"You know I hate it when you beg." Sarah sighed.

"I can't help it! It's making my mouth water!" Addie shot back.

"At least pretend you're a normal dog with manners?" Sarah requested.

Addie looked forlorn, but complied by returning to her spot at the foot of the dining table.

Sarah and Eli tucked into their food. Eli hesitantly raised the first forkful to his mouth, testing it with the tip of his tongue, then murmured with appreciation when he realized it tasted pretty good. He nodded approvingly at Sarah and began to chow down. Sarah beamed, proud of herself.

As they finished their meal and talked about their respective days, Sarah realized that she loved this little life they had. It was these simple, unexciting moments that made her realize how lucky she truly was. There wasn't a single thing she loathed about Eli. Everything was peaceful and easy. Remarkably easy. They either agreed or talked out their differences and reached a solution. They didn't argue; they didn't dither. They spent most of their time in an easy, peaceful, companionable contentment—enjoying every day, every date, and every inside joke.

She started to run the dishwater in the sink while Eli cleared the dishes. He stood beside her as they washed the dishes together, occasionally flicking soapy water at each other and laughing. The kitchen was so small that they constantly bumped into each other whenever they tried to do anything in it.

Technically Michael Howler's house was all Sarah's, but she shared it with Eli almost every night, and she loved that. An idea suddenly occurred to Sarah: *I wonder if Eli would want to move in with me?*

It seemed crazy that she had not thought of it before. They spent nearly every night together and ate almost every meal together, so what was the point of paying two separate housing bills? After all, Eli still had to pay rent on his tiny place, as well as utilities. In addition, there was the inconvenience of deciding where to sleep each night and packing items to take to his place, or him packing items to bring to hers. They had both left clothes and essentials in each other's homes, but it seemed a bit ridiculous at this point to keep switching back and forth.

But how do I ask? she then thought. *What if he says*

no or freaks out? The men I know hate rushing into things.

"*Why would he say no?*" Addie piped up, filling Sarah's mind with her telepathic voice.

Sarah smiled down at Addie. "*Would you like him to live with us?*" she responded.

"*Absolutely! I love Eli!*" Addie answered. To emphasize her point, she hopped up and began to bark excitedly and wag her tail.

"What is it, girl?" Eli asked her, petting her back.

She sat down and looked at him adoringly.

"Want to go for a walk?" Eli asked.

She hopped up again, barking frantically with joy. Eli and Sarah smiled at each other and held hands as they accompanied Addie into the woods for a short evening walk.

GET YOUR COPY NOW
http://getbook.at/pawtrayal

DISCOVER
THE SPELLWOOD WITCHES SERIES

———

WITCH'S TAIL, BOOK 1

Can she awaken her dormant powers and stop a desperate killer destroying the forest? If you like paranormal puzzles, delightful canine companions, and environmental enlightenment, then you'll love Melanie Snow's wagging-ly fun whodunit.

Here's the link to buy the book today!
http://getbook.at/witchstail

HOWL PLAY, BOOK 2

A novice witch. A collie companion. Can this clever duo put noses to the ground to chase down a killer? If you like cute flirty romance, discovering one's true destiny, and love for animals, then you'll adore Melanie Snow's barking-ly fun adventure.

Here's the link to buy the book today!
http://getbook.at/howlplay

TAIL OF A FEATHER, BOOK 3

A mysterious portal. Eight crows with a message. A missing police chief. If you like paranormal puzzles, charming canine companions, and a bit of flirty romance, then you will love Melanie Snow's crafty quest. Take flight into the magical world of Witchland.

Here's the link to buy the book today!
http://getbook.at/tailofafeather

IMPAWSIBLE MISCHIEF, BOOK 4

Stolen charms. A mysterious woman running for mayor. Can beginner's magic save an ill-fated land? If you like wisecracking creatures, enchanting characters, and close-knit sisterhoods, then you'll love Melanie Snow's clever story.

Here's the link to buy the book today!
http://getbook.at/impawsiblemischief

PAWTRAYAL, BOOK 5

When a ghost cries murder, an unsolved case could cost her future. Can this witch solve the magical mystery when an old enemy starts casting chaos. If you like wise familiars, heartthrob romances, and mystical whodunits, then you'll love Melanie Snow's paranormal brainteaser.

Here's the link to buy the book today
http://getbook.at/pawtrayal

Don't Miss Your Free Gift!

Thank you for purchasing *Impawsible Mischief, The Spellwood Witches, Book 4.* To show my appreciation and because of a popular request from my readers I am offering a:

Welcome to Witchland Map

https://wendyvandepoll.com/melaniesnowgift

Join Melanie Snow's Paranormal Cozy Mystery Facebook Group

The Wolf Coven

https://www.facebook.com/
groups/melaniesnowcozymysteries

About Melanie Snow

Melanie Snow is the pen name for Wendy Van de Poll, a bestselling author, pet loss grief coach, and animal medium. She is the author of The Spellwood Witches, a paranormal cozy mystery series.

Her books weave together positive magic, snarky forest faeries, and insightful animals with fun and eclectic humor. True life adventures and intuition are woven into her stories laced with unbridled imagination.

She has been followed by wild wolves in minus sixty degrees, hissed at by a mama bobcat, and played ball with a wild owl—among other animal encounters.

Find out more about her work by visiting her on her website https://wendyvandepoll.com/melanie-snow.

Also get *The Welcome to Witchland Map.*

Download Your Free Gift

https://wendyvandepoll.com/melaniesnowgift

HOW TO FIND MELANIE SNOW

www.wendyvandepoll.com/melanie-snow

www.facebook.com/melaniesnow.cozymysteries

www.instagram.com/melaniesnow.cozymysteries

www.facebook.com/
groups/melaniesnowcozymysteries

www.amazon.com/author/melaniesnow

www.goodreads.com/melaniesnowcozymysteries

ACKNOWLEDGEMENTS

I would like to thank my intuitive writing team who has guided me to write this fun series. They weren't always easy to deal with but they were patient with my fumbling. Because of them Melanie Snow and all the characters in my head have come to life.

I appreciate all my teachers of the furred, feathered, and finned variety who continue to guide me through life and teach me what matters.

A special thanks goes to my weekly writing buddies H.R. Hobbs and Toni Crowe who are kind, sassy, and amazing authors.

I offer a tremendous amount of appreciation to my beta readers: Nadine, Vicky, and Renee. To my editor

Robyn Margaret Verdugo a huge thank you for your expertise. And thank you to my talented proofreader Allison Rose.

A huge hug goes to my husband, Rick Van de Poll. He is a remarkable poet and human being who dedicates his life to the animals and the environment. He inspires my soul. You can find his books on Amazon, as well.

And of course, Addie. This rescue puppy flew on a jet plane from Texas to grace my life in many ways and writing books with her as a main character is just one. Addie even has her own series called; The Adventures of Ms. Addie Pants on Amazon.